Profyle Bytes

By
E.A. Lopez

Harrison House Publishing
San Antonio, Texas

Profyle Bytes
All Rights Reserved
Copyright © 2011 E. A. Lopez
v2.0
Edited by R. L. Sloan
Cover Art designed by J. Alexander, Genesis Productions©
some cover images are courtesy of www.freedigitalphotos.net

Harrison House Publishing
www.theharrisonhousepublishing.com
info@theharrisonhousepublising.com
Paperback ISBN: 978-1-4507-5156-8
Library of Congress Control Number: 2011944068
Harrison House Publishing and the "HHP" logo are trademarks belonging to Harrison House Publishing.

PRINTED IN THE UNITED STATES OF AMERICA

For the three people who have never given up on me...MOM, DAD, and JAM.

ACKNOWLEDGEMENTS

I would like to thank my family and friends who have been there, supported, and believed in me through my journey in writing this novel. I wish to thank God for blessing me with so many beautiful people in my life and giving me the strength to carry on and the ability to overcome all obstacles. A special thanks to my very good friend, Rhonda Sloan, who not only mentored me, but encouraged, and supported me through the process of my writing. Thank you my friend, I appreciate everything you have done for me.

A very special thanks to my great friend, Jamaar Milner, who has inspired me in so many ways, and is the inspiration that started it all in my first short story and poem. I will never be able to repay what you have done for me, but I will try everyday for the rest of my life, thank you. A special thanks to my children, who have kept me laughing through the years, I love you all. Lastly, but not least, I need to thank the two people who brought me into this world, my mom and my dad. Dad, may you rest in peace, you are missed. Mom, I want to thank you and Lisa for everything you have both done for me, your love has been unconditional, and it's the most precious thing I have in life.

CHAPTER ONE

Waking up that night in a cold sweat was unlike any of the other nights that I awoke from dreams. I didn't know exactly what to make of it. As soon as I turned to look at the clock to check the time, my cell phone rang. I knew it was AJ by the ring tone that played.

"Hey girl, what up?" I said half asleep.

AJ's voice was in a panic state. I couldn't understand what she was saying.

"What's wrong, slow down, I'm not understandin' ya girl."

"Nova, have you heard from Geminiah tonight?"

"No, I haven't seen that girl since passing her by on the way to class this morning. Come to think of it, she didn't call me and let me know how her thing went." I didn't understand what this was all about.

"AJ, what's going on?"

"I can't believe her mom hasn't called you since you two are tight." AJ's voice shook with fear.

"I don't think Mrs. Carmichael called me, at least I didn't hear my phone." I tried to process what was with all the questions.

"AJ, girl, if you don't get to the point... It's 3 a.m. and I have to get to the gym in a few hours," I yawned, still half asleep.

"Nova, Nia's missing," AJ replied.

Nia is the sister name we called Geminiah because she didn't like her government name as she so put it. She said it made her feel different and she didn't like to be an outcast.

"Please girl, she's prolly still out havin' a good time." I put a chuckle in my voice, to lighten the mood.

"No Nova, Nia didn't make it home for the weekend. You know she always visits with her mom. I got a text from Jules about twenty minutes ago. Jules got a call from Mrs. Carmichael wondering if Nia was at the sorority house or if anyone knew of her where abouts."

AJ sounded upset with me because I was not taking the conversation seriously. I told AJ I would call her right back. She knew I was going to call Nia. I was the one person that Nia would not push the ignore button if I called. If she was having a good time and just didn't want to be bothered, she would still pick up for me. We had that type of connection.

I didn't say anything to Aleea because I wasn't sure how much she knew, but Nia had planned to meet a guy she met online. Nia had a boyfriend, but she was having issues with him. I didn't like him much, but I kept quiet about it, because she really liked him. We all knew he was a jerk. When he hadn't called her in a month, I told her to move on. She finally did, and I was happy about it. She tried to tell me about the guy she met online. I saw her in one of the University halls earlier that day, but I was in a rush because I was late for class. My professor had already warned me about being late to his class again. I told her I would talk with her later that day, but I didn't see her again on campus. I didn't think anything of it, because I knew I would see her back at the sorority house later that night before she left for the weekend to go home.

I picked up my phone to dial Nia's number. A cold chill came over me. I had never experienced the sudden coldness that came over me before and couldn't explain it. I suddenly felt as if something was terribly wrong. My hand started to shake as I dialed her number. Her call tone started to play. I was worried, but that call tone of hers put a smile on my face. The music started to play... "Everything's gonna be okay, Just Dance."

That call tone truly describes Nia's whole attitude toward life. The girl loves to dance. It didn't matter where or when, she is always ready to dance. I think that's the connection she has to AJ. AJ also loves to dance. She's always doing some happy dance in the common area. The music came to a sudden stop as her voicemail came on...

"I'm either on the other line, away from my phone, or just not answering. Either way you're not important. (Her giggle) Just kidding, you know what to do."

My stomach dropped because Nia always answered when I called, even when we were mad at one another. Fear raced through my heart as I choked on the message I left...

"Hey girl, this is not cool, you have everybody worried. Why aren't you answering your phone? Get back to me ASAP. And Nia, you don't hear me laughing. You better not be ignoring this damn call. Hit me up on the text. Your mother is about to send out the search party. A'ight girl."

I pushed the end button. Thoughts went racing through my head. Just then my phone rang. I immediately thought it was Nia calling me back, but I realized it wasn't her ring tone. It was my default tone.

"Hello."

"Nova, I have been trying to reach you all night. Why haven't you answered your phone young lady?"

She said in a stern tone that made me feel like I was nine years old again.

"Hi, Mrs. Carmichael, I'm sorry I was fast asleep. I didn't realize you were calling. I apologize." My voice sounded low.

Nia's mother was the only other person, besides my own mom, who could make me feel like a child even though I'm an adult---a twenty-two year old adult.

"Have you heard from Geminiah? She was supposed to come this weekend for a visit as she always does, but she has not arrived. She always calls if she is going to arrive late," she asked. I could hear the worry in her voice.

"No Ma'am, I haven't talk to Nia, I mean Geminiah, since this morning. I saw her, but I was late for my English Lit class and we had a couple of words, but that's it."

"Why does it sound like you're not telling me something Nova?" she said accusingly.

"I'm not sure what you are insinuating Mrs. Carmichael? Why would I not tell you something?" I said with my voice shaking as it usually does when I'm holding something back.

Nia's mother sounded furious through her breath as she was listening to me babble through my words.

"Listen here Missy. I'm worried about my daughter. If you know where she is at, you better spill it." After catching herself, Ms. Carmichael calmed down.

"I'm sorry Nova. I don't mean to hold you responsible for Geminiah, but I'm truly worried about her. This is not like her. She's my only child. Please Nova, if you know where she might be..." She couldn't continue as she sobbed.

I knew about the online date, but I didn't want to tell Mrs. Carmichael yet. Nia would kill me if I told her mother she went to meet a total stranger. We were more than friends, we were sorority sister. We kept each other's secrets no matter what. I could not betray the oath we had taken. I would have to hold my tongue and see if she returned home. If she didn't, then I would have no choice, but to break our oath.

"Are you listening to me Nova?" she said.

"I'm sorry, Mrs. Carmichael. Yes, I am listening. I tried to call Geminiah. She didn't answer her phone. It's not like her to do that. I left her a message. She hasn't returned my call. She hasn't even text me," I replied as the reality hit me that Nia could be in real trouble.

"I'm calling the police." Frantic and distraught, she did what any parent would do.

"Alright, Mrs. Carmichael, I'm on my way over. I'll be there shortly." I hung up the phone.

I rushed to get my clothes, so I could get dressed, and I remembered I told AJ I would call her back. I dialed AJ's number. We each had a call tone that in some way described our personality. AJ's was a song from the 90's. That girl was all about the 90's. She answered.

"Hey, did you get a hold of her?"

"Naw, she didn't answer. Look, ya know that Nia wouldn't do a disappearin' act or not call. I'm worried."

"I'm on my way to her Mother's house. Call the sisters, each of us needs to be there. Make sure that everyone understands. Be there within an hour," I said as I rushed AJ off the phone before she could say anything.

I rushed over to my dresser and pulled out a t-shirt and jeans. My phone rang. It was AJ.

"Yes, AJ," I answered with a slight tone of attitude.

"Nova, do I inform all the sisters or just us... You know

what I mean," she said.

"Just us, AJ, no one else in the sorority needs to know. Not yet anyways," I replied.

Even though we belonged to a large sorority, eight of us are tight with each other. We did just about everything together. Four of us pledged the sorority at the same time. Nia, Julie, Emerald and I pledged our Freshman year. Sonariah and Trinity were sophomores when we pledged. They were already hanging with Luna. Luna was a junior at the time. She is the oldest sister amongst us. Then, there is Aleea Johnson, aka AJ. She's the baby sister of the click. She just pledged this year as an incoming freshman. We took her in immediately because she was Jules' younger biological half-sister. They had the same father. As a younger sibling, she received immediate membership into the sorority. AJ stood tall at 5' 11 inches. She had a deep brown skin tone, very pretty, very thin, but she could eat. No one could ever guess that by looking at her though. I don't know if she was bi-racial like Julie, but she looked black.

I never would have guessed in a million years that I would be part of a sorority, yet part of a sisterhood. As a teenager, in high school, I hung out with the wrong crowd and found myself in all sorts of trouble. I dated a guy that not only used drugs, but he sold them at the high school. I didn't know any better. He broke up with me. I was devastated at the time. Now, looking back it was probably the best thing he could have done for me.

I immediately hooked up with another guy. He was a transfer from another high school in the area. Although, San Antonio, Texas is big it's also very small. I met him through a friend that I went to middle school with. We dated throughout high school. I thought I was in love with him. What dumb teenage girl doesn't think she is in love with her boyfriend during high school? I broke up with him right after graduation. Never gave him an explanation, but I knew we were wrong for each other.

I went directly into the workforce after graduation. I didn't think college would be right for me. I tried a couple of entry-level positions, but I had some trouble being told what to do. I met a girl, Anna, at the last job I attempted. She was in college part-time. She would come into work and talk about college life. One after-noon, I sat with her at lunch and just talked. By the end of the day, I decided that I would give college a try.

I applied to the University of San Antonio. To my own amazement, I was accepted. It's not that I was dumb; I just learned how to get by in high school. I didn't think that I could do the same in college. I think that's what scared me the most. However, due to a late registration, I didn't have time to re-think the situation.

A week before classes, I had to report to the campus for student orientation and dorm assignments. I still remember how boring student orientation was. I sat next to a couple of girls who were getting on my nerves. They wouldn't shut up. They kept go-ing on about their hair, make-up and shoes. Not to mention, the numerous giggles as they talked. These were the kind of girls that I tried to stay away from in high school. I finally just got up and tried to move slowly to the back of the lecture room.

As I moved, one of the girls rolled her eyes and made a smart-ass comment under her breath. I couldn't make out what she said, but I was about to call her on it. I'm not one to let anyone put me down. Just as I turned around and started to make my way back toward them, I heard someone say, "Don't pay any attention to them, they have no clue."

She was a very pretty girl. She had blonde hair and green

eyes. She was very thin, and stood about 5' 7 inches tall. She was the American version of the girl next door. If I didn't know better, I'd swear I was talking to a life-size Barbie.

She smiled and said, "Come sit over here with us."
I didn't smile back and really didn't know what to make of her invitation, but I went along seeing that I didn't know anyone else in the room.

She said, "I'm Geminiah and this is Julie, and Emerald."
"I'm Nova."

"Nova, that's a cool name. Do you mind me asking how you came about that name," Geminiah asked.

I said with a smirk on my face, "It's a long story, so the short version goes like this…

"My mother was supposed to get a 1976 Chevy Nova for her 16th birthday, but she got PG instead. My grandparents, at the time were upset, and decided to use the money for the car to buy the things I was going to need when I was born. Out of spite and rebellion, my mother showed them, she got the last laugh, and named me "NOVA".

"Wow, how cool is that?" Geminiah laughed.

She had this strange laugh that sounded kind of like a mixture between a giggle and laugh that was just evil. Whatever it was, I knew, right there and then, we would be tight.

Julie and Emerald on the other hand took a little while to get to know. We really didn't become good friends until our second year in college. Julie Johnson, aka Jules, was very pretty. Bi-racial with mocha-colored skin, she had an athletic figure, long black hair and was about 5' 6 inches tall. She was the type of girl that was always in the gym. The type of girl, if you didn't know her, you hated because she was always eating right and exercising. She had all the guys after her, but she was serious about college and wouldn't give most of them the time of day. She and Emerald had been best friends throughout high school.

Emerald Mills, aka Em, was also very pretty. She had a dark brown skin tone. The sunlight would glisten off her skin. She always kept her hair neat and in style. The girl truly had class. African-American, 6 feet tall and very slender, Emerald had a beautiful smile. Her and Jules were inseparable. Their first year of college, they took all the same classes. Eventually, their majors had them go separate direction, but they remained as tight as can be.

They all knew what they wanted to major in since day one of college. Nia wanted to go into teaching, so she majored in Education. She loved children and wanted several of her own someday. Em was a business major. She knew she was going to be CEO of a major corporation. As for Jules, she was the artistic one of the bunch. Her major was in Art. She planned to have her own art exhibition one day. As for me, my major was undeclared my first year of college. I just wanted to get through my first year without any issues.

My first semester of college was rough. I was glad that I had each of them for a class. They kept me focused and I was truly grateful for that. There were several times that I wanted to give up and quit. They wouldn't allow it. Nia suggested that we join a sorority. Em and Jules were all for it. I, on the other hand, did not think it was a good idea. They would fit in perfectly---they were pretty, smart, and knew what they wanted. They oozed confidence. I never really thought of myself as pretty. I knew I wasn't ugly, but I just didn't think I was cut out to be sorority material.

Nia convinced me that I had just as much to offer as they did. She said they didn't hang with ugly girls or girls that lacked self-esteem. She said I fit perfectly into their little click. I laughed. Nia is very outspoken. Sometimes she says things without giving it a thought, but the girl doesn't care---that's just her. Em and Jules confirmed what she said, but I think they did it because Nia was their friend. So, we went out to a sorority party during rush week.

It was hard at first. I was a little intimidated by all the pretty girls. They all looked like Nia with blonde hair and blue or green eyes. They all had petite figures and filled with attitude. One girl headed in our direction and she introduced herself to us.

"Hi, I'm Briana."

Even though she introduced herself, we immediately knew that she was talking to Nia. Em, Jules, and I looked at each other because she totally dismissed us. Nia realized it to and replied to her with a polite "hey". We started to walk toward the door when this group of girls came toward us. They were all of color. When I say color, I mean women of color who are Latina, African-American, Native-American, etc. They were pretty, and dressed very nicely. One of them in the group spoke to us.

"Hey Girls, are you here to check out the sorority?"

Her name was Luna Gonzalez. She was Latina, had light brown skin, and short dark brown hair styled very nicely. She had a cute curvy figure, hazel eyes and stood 5' 8 inches tall. She displayed sophistication. You could tell that her hair and nail got serviced at a salon. She was a junior and a political science major. There were two other girls standing beside her.

Trinity Howard, aka Tee, was African-American and appeared friendly. She was gorgeous---slender with curves as well. She had a medium brown skin tone and golden brown eyes with a hint of green. She wore a high ponytail, but you could tell she took care of her hair. She was 5'5 inches tall. A sophomore, Trinity was the one that we all would envy later. Intelligent and well put together, Trinity presented as pretty, pre-med, and had a boyfriend that was a star quarterback at the university across town.

Sonariah Reyes, aka Rae-Rae, was Latina and pretty. With medium-length dark brown, wavy hair, she stood thin with a light brown complexion and brown eyes. She was 5' 7 inches tall. She could have been a comedian. She always cracked jokes from the minute we met her. A sophomore and a psychology major, Sonariah had a boyfriend she had been with since high school. She was down to earth and had a unique laugh.

They all actually seemed to be down to earth. Even though they appeared to be like the other girls in the sorority, something was different about them. It wasn't until I really looked around the room and noticed that we all were the only women of color present throughout the sorority house. I think Trinity caught on to my observation as my eyes scanned the room. She came over to me and whispered.

"Hey, chill out. You're definitely sorority material."
I didn't quite understand what Trinity meant that night, but I found out later when we became good friends.

We had a great time at the party. We left that night excited. I didn't tell any of them what Trinity had said to me. I didn't want to jinx our chances, so I kept my mouth shut about it. We started to walk back to our dorm rooms. We all lived on campus and got lucky enough to get housed on the same floor of Chisholm Hall. It seemed like fate had played a part in our meeting and becoming friends. Em and Jules were roommates, of course, and Nia lived two doors down from me.

We had to walk all the way across campus to get back to our dorms. The campus was huge, yet they were still expanding because enrollment had doubled in the last five years. Jules wanted to jog back. We looked at her like she was crazy, but then again she was the exercise guru. We convinced her that if she walked back with us we would all exercise with her on a regular basis at the university's gym. She got that look in her eyes then she started talking about an exercise program that she would put together for each of us. Then, she started talking about dieting. Nia broke out laughing so hard and said, "Girl, I need my Mexican food!" We all started laughing. We clicked together, but it wouldn't be until later that we realized why and how.

We got back to the dorms after a long walk. Jules and Em went to their room, which was down the hall. Nia and I walked over to our rooms.

"Hey Nia, Thanks!"

"For what crazy?" she replied.

"For talking me into this sorority thing, it could be the highlight of our college days," I said with a smile.

"Girl, the sorority is just the beginning. Before we graduate from this university, we are gonna rule it and cause some chaos along the way." She smiled, laughed, and walked into her room.

I stood outside my door for minute before I walked into my room. My roommate was sound asleep. She was sort of cool, but a bit nerdy. She was always reading a book, not like there's anything wrong with that, but she didn't appear to have an outside life because her education was so important to her. She was Latina, and the only person I knew that was shorter than me. She stood 5 feet tall, with a medium built and very pretty. She had a natural brown tan and was tan year round and I envied that. Her hair was medium-length, straight, and jet-black. She had deep dark brown eyes, and was very smart. The girl was there on a full ride academically.

I was just glad that we got along because I was going to room with her for the semester.

      With all the excitement and the adrenaline rushing through my body, I couldn't sleep. I knew I had to try to get some rest. I laid down on the bed and closed my eyes. I tossed and turned for a good while, but finally nodded off to only be awoken by a strange feeling. I didn't know what it was. I remember opening my eyes and realizing that I was swinging my arms around as if I was trying to fight someone off of me. Funny thing is that no one, other than my roommate, was in the room. I felt a presence that was so strong, but I couldn't see anyone or anything there with me. It took me a while to get back to sleep that night, but I finally did after convincing myself that it was all a bad dream.

CHAPTER TWO

The next morning I awoke to a loud banging on the door. I could hear Nia laughing as she was yelling for me to wake my ass up. I rushed to open the door.

"Girl, you're gonna wake everyone and their mommas up," I whispered.

I looked over to my roommate to see if she had woken up from the noise. Her bed was already made and she was nowhere in sight.

"Get dressed so we can head over to the bookstore before they run out of the books I need for class. I mean the books we need for class." Nia said with a giggle.

She pushed her way pass me and jumped on my bed.

"Hurry up!" She said.

"Dang girl, give me a minute!" I rushed over to my dresser and pulled out some sweat pants and a t-shirt.

Nia and I decided to walk over to the bookstore instead of driving. It was a nice day out and she wanted to check out the scenery as she put it. We decided after we purchased our books that we would go grab something to eat at the cafeteria. On our way to the bookstore, Nia's eye fell on something very interesting--well, someone very interesting.

"Hey," she said with a smile.

A group of guys walked by us. I looked at her.

"Hey cutie," he replied to her.

"Can you tell me how to get to the book store from here?"

she asked.

I grinned because we both knew where the bookstore was.

"It's not too far. You go down that direction and by the English building make a left, then go across the bridge and into the student facility, then down the stairs and your there."

A very good-looking guy, later I would realize that he was exactly Nia's type. He was Latino, muscular in all the right places with short dark brown hair that was faded out. He had a nice smile and voice that would make any girl get goose bumps.

"I'm confused. So, you go down make a left, at which building, then across where. Huh?" she said as she turned to me and winked.

"Maybe I should just walk you two over there," he answered with a smile.

"That would be nice, right Nova?"

"Is this where the computer labs are?" I said.

"Yes," he replied.

"Hey Geminiah, I'm gonna head on to the computer lab. I need to check my email, and other things. You go ahead and I'll meet you at the cafeteria in about an hour." I said as I winked backed at her.

As I walked off, I could hear Nia giggling. She was funny. I walked into the building and looked around for a while before searching for the computer lab. I found the lab shortly after making my way around. I walked in and sat down at one of the computers. I tried logging on, but it wouldn't allow me to. I looked around to find help, but no one was around that was working there. All of sudden, I hear a voice say,

"Didn't you go to freshman orientation? You need to use your social as the password for the first time you log in."

He was sitting directly in front of me.

"How do you know this is my first time logging in?" I re-plied with an attitude because he was up in my business.

"Whatever, I was just trying to help you out, but since you know how to log in, my bad." He said with a laugh.

I didn't know who he was, but I knew that he was getting on my last nerve, and I didn't like people in my personal space.

"Go ahead, since you know how to log in, use your social for the password. I'm sure you just forgot about that freshman," he said.

"Excuse me, you just assume that I'm a freshman," I said.

"My bad, I guess I'm jumping to conclusions again," he said as he laughed harder this time. "I'm Maxwell."

Before he could finish introducing himself, I got up and moved to another computer. He was the first person I met on campus of the opposite sex and he was annoying me. He was a good-looking guy for someone that was annoying. He stood about 5'9 inches tall. He had a deep dark chocolate skin tone, with an athletic build. He was wearing a wife beater, so you could see his biceps. He had a great smile that showed off his pearly whites. He had black eyes and wore his hair in dreads. He was not my type at all. The usual guy that I found myself attracted to was the clean-cut bad boy type.

Sitting in front of the computer, I did what he said. I used my social for the password, and online access was now avail-able to me. I smiled. I looked up to see if he saw, but as I looked his way, he turned quickly. I did notice the grin that came upon his face. I logged onto my email and checked it. I saw that I had several messages from my social networks. I had accounts with MyProfyle, YourIt, and Friendbook. I immediately logged on to

MyProfyle. I had several messages from friends, but one message jump out at me immediately. It was from the mystery man that I had been talking to through messages for the past month. I didn't know what he looked liked because he didn't have a picture on his profile. It was awkward not knowing who I was talking to and to also know that he knew exactly what I looked like from the pictures I had posted.

I opened the messages. It read...

Hey wat up? Wat r u getting into this weekend?

A smile came over my face as I wrote back to him. I replied by telling him I was not sure what I was going to be doing that weekend. Then I read all my other messages and comments. I was going to sign off when I noticed a reply from him. I opened it. His message read...

Well maybe we could chill.

Although I wanted to reply with a yes, I knew I didn't know him, nor did I know what he looked like, and again, I didn't know him. So, I hit reply and sent the following message:

Hmmm... maybe if I knew u. LOL

I looked at the clock and realized that I had to meet Nia soon. I logged off my account and ended my session on the computer.

"Don't forget to log off your computer. You don't want somebody else using your account." He said in a sarcastic tone.

I rolled my eyes, got up, and left the lab. I didn't say a word, not a "thanks", or a "good-bye", or even a "nice meeting you".

As I proceeded to walk over to the cafeteria, I had several thoughts running through my mind. I really wanted to meet the mystery man, but what if he was some psycho, pervert or, even

worse, a serial killer? That was the only problem with meeting
people online through social networks. You never knew if they
really were who they said they were. I also thought about the guy,
Maxwell, from the computer lab. Even though he was annoying,
he was attractive. I wonder if I would see him again on campus. I
didn't even know if he went to the university.

I had to walk through the courtyard in order to get to the
cafeteria. There was a huge water fountain in the middle of the
campus. You could hear the water running. The sound from it was
so refreshing. I walked down the steps and approached the cafete-
ria. I didn't see Nia anywhere in sight. I decided to have a seat and
wait to see if she showed up. After a short while, I figured she was
still with that guy she met, the cute looking Latino. I decided to get
a bite to eat. I walked over to the food line, and then I heard her
laugh. She was walking in through the door.

"Hey Girl, what, you couldn't wait for me to eat?" she
laughed.

"My bad, I just got hungry, besides, I been waitin' on ya for
'bout 20 minutes."

"Well this is Marco," she replied.

"Hey Marco, nice to meet ya," I said while looking at her
and raising an eyebrow.

They both walked over to the food line and proceeded to
order lunch. I decided to have a sandwich, chips and a drink.

"Let's sit outside in the courtyard. It's nice out," I said to
Nia.

"Alright girl, that's cool."

I carried my food out with me, while Nia had Marco carry
theirs. The girl had only been on campus for a couple of weeks and
she already had a man doing things for her.

"So, did you find the computer lab?" Nia asked.

"Yep, and I got all my email checked including those on MyProfyle."

"You got a MyProfyle? I do too. I'll have to add you as a friend. What's your screen name?"

"DarkAngel," I replied.

We both laughed. Marco didn't say a word, just like a typical guy, he was munching down his lunch.

After lunch, Nia said her good-bye to Marco. They exchanged numbers. We started walking back to our dorm. Nia asked me what I thought about Marco. I told her that he was a good-looking guy and seemed nice. She said that he asked her to hang out the following night. He wanted her to meet him at a club downtown. She asked if I could go with her, since he was going to be there with his buddies. She suggested that maybe he could introduce me to one of them, seeing that I didn't have a boyfriend.

"I'll go with you Nia, but I don't need you to hook me up. I've been talking to someone online. He asked me what I was doing this weekend. Maybe I should invite him out to that club. It would be safe since it's a public place. Right?" I said to her trying to convince myself more than I was trying to convince her.

"Yea, whatever girl," Nia had a blank look on her face as she appeared to be in her own world.

"Oh yea, I met some jerk at the lab. His name is Maxwell. He was very cute, but so freakin' annoying," I said hoping that she heard me.

"Maxwell, isn't that a last name? So, what class is he?" she replied.

"I don't know. I didn't ask him much. Like I said, he was getting on my nerves. Maybe I will see him again on campus," I

said as we entered the door to the building of our dorm.

"Any plans tonight?" she asked.

"Naw, none solid anyway. Do you have anything going on tonight?"

"I wish, but I have to go visit my mom. I'll probably stay the night there. I'll be back tomorrow though, so you better be ready to go to the club. We'll leave around 11 p.m. Okay!" She said as she turned to walk into her room.

"A'ight, girl, but call me if you change your plans. Don't wanna be waitin' 'round on ya," I said with a slight grin on my face.

She knew I was hinting at the fact that she left me waiting on her earlier.

I entered my room. My roommate was at her desk. She was reading a book.

"Hey, what are you reading?" I asked.

"Just getting a jump start on some of my classes," she replied.

"Oh, I see. Well, cool."

"Any plans for tonight?" I asked as if I was hinting that maybe she should take a break from the books since it was Friday.

"Just reading all weekend." She turned the page of her book.

She never looked at me once while our short conversation took place. I sat down on my bed. It didn't take much longer to realize that the silence in the room was going to drive me crazy. I decided to go back to the computer lab and do some social networking online.

I wanted to see more of the campus, so I took another route. The campus was beautiful. You could automatically tell which buildings were new and which ones had been standing for a while. I entered the building. I don't know if my intentions were to use the computer lab or to see if I would run into Maxwell again. Either way, I was walking into the lab before you knew it. I looked around. There were several people using the computers, but Maxwell was not in sight. I was a little disappointed, but I soon put it in the back of my mind and logged on to MyProfyle. There was a notification on my page that I had unread messages. I went to my inbox. There was a message from the mystery man, aka NC Kidd. NC Kidd was his screen name. I smiled as I opened the message. It read...

Well, u might get to know me if we chilled sometime. Here's my number, 872-6235. Call me r hit me up on the txt.

My first thought was to pick up my cell and call him, but I was a bit scared. He seemed cool and caught my interest somehow, but I didn't know if I wanted to take the risk. It was strange because I've always considered myself a risk-taker, except when it came to dating and relationships. I was a closed book when it came to that. Ever since the break-up in high school I had a wall built around me, so that no one could ever get close enough to hurt me.

I knew I had to reply to his message, but wasn't sure if I was going to call him. I sent him a message telling him I would give him a call sometime and left it at that. I went onto the other two social networking sites that I had accounts for. I didn't go on to those sites as much as I did on this one. I checked messages, but nothing exciting was there. I logged off the computer after a couple of hours at the lab. The sun was starting to go down slowly and I knew I didn't want to be walking around campus in the dark, so I head back to my dorm room.

As I got to the building, my phone rang. I had no clue who could be calling me since few people had my number.

"Hello."

"Hey girl, it's me. What are you doing?" Nia said in a high-pitched voice.

"Headin' back to the dorm and you?"

"Going crazy here at the house. I can't get Marco off my mind. You know what I mean. I can't wait to see him tomorrow. You are going with me downtown, right? You haven't changed your mind, have you? I need you to be there tomorrow night Nova."

Nia went on as if she had not talked to me in days. I laughed jokingly.

"Slow down girl. Dang, you excited. What ya on?"

"It's a natural high," she replied.

We stayed on the phone for a while as she went on and on about Marco. Nia was all about Nia. Don't get me wrong. She is a very good friend, but a horrible listener. She's a natural talker. She loses interest after listening for a while, but that's how we became such good friends because I'm a natural listener and problem solver. I told Nia about NC Kidd and that he gave me his number. She suggested that I call him and then she went back to discussing Marco. I could only take so much of one subject, so I told her that I was going to jump in the shower and get some sleep. We said our good-byes and I told her that I would see her tomorrow when she got back to the dorm.

I don't like lying to people, especially friends, so I did jump in the shower. The one personality trait that I hate most in people is lying. It's because I have been lied to so much in my life, so much in fact, that I can sniff out a liar instantly. I guess that's a talent that has grown with me over the years.

I had planned to sleep after my shower, but my roommate had her lamp on and was still reading. The slightest bit of light is enough to keep me up. I laid down on my bed and was looking up at the ceiling when it hit me. I had not used NC Kidd's number. I grabbed my cell from my nightstand. I went into my contacts and hit the text button. The screen came up. I entered a text saying...

"Hey, it's DarkAngel, how r u tonite?"

I pushed the send button. I panicked and tried to push the end button before the message could be sent but it was too late. Away the message went.

It took a couple of minutes before he replied. My text ring tone played. I was nervous but happy that he sent a text back. His text read,

"Im good Angel, jus chillin'. What r u doin?"

I smiled and replied to his text. I told him that I was doing the same thing. This time he replied immediately,

"So what r u gettin' in2 tmr nite."

I couldn't believe that I replied to him by telling him that I was going out to a club downtown. The text ring tone went off again. He replied by asking which club was I going to. The text went back and forth for about an hour. We both were asking questions of each other and answering.

By the end of the night, I felt as if I actually knew NC Kidd. The only exception to that was that I still had no idea what he looked like. Although in his defense, he did tell me that he was African-American and a college student. He was also a year younger than me, so I put two and two together and assumed he was a freshman. Most freshmen were a year or two younger than me since I took a year and a half off after graduating from high school. Nia, Em, and Jules were all a year younger than me.

My roommate finally turned off the light and went to bed. I closed my eyes, but couldn't sleep for two very specific reasons. NC Kidd was on my mind and I also couldn't help but remember my dream from the night before. Before long, I was fast asleep. My mind was racing a hundred miles an hour. Dreams kept coming and going. I couldn't make sense of any of them.

I was lying on my stomach. My arms were crossed and on my pillow as my head lay upon them. All of sudden, a coldness came over me and goose bumps formed on my body. I felt someone holding down my arms. I couldn't get my eyes to open. I tried to scream, but the sound wasn't coming out. I could hear myself trying to scream louder for someone to help me. I felt as if someone was lying on top of me, touching my body, and I couldn't get them off. I kept pleading for it to stop. I begged while I tried to free my arms. I heard a horrible growling noise from whatever it was. My eyes finally opened and I focused them. As suddenly as it came on, it was gone.

I turned over and sat up on the bed. I was shaking. I turned on the lamp sitting on the nightstand. I looked over to my roommate. She was sound asleep. I thought to myself no one could have slept through that. The presence was stronger than the time before and felt so real. I kept thinking it was too real to be a dream, but what else could it have been? I left the light on the rest of that night. I couldn't fall back to sleep until I saw the sunlight come through the window.

I slept in that Saturday morning. My roommate must have thought I was a night person or just lazy. I awoke to the sound of my text ring tone. It was NC Kidd. He sent me a text saying he hoped I had a great day. I smiled and instantly thought that was cool. I replied saying I hoped the same for him. He replied, asking if I was still going out to the club downtown. I sent a text back informing him that I was. He replied letting me know that he wanted to meet me there. I hesitated for a minute, and then sent him a text saying I would see him at the club. The responses stopped.

I was excited, but also curious if I would know who he was when I saw him. I still had no idea what he looked like, but knew he would find me. My mind suddenly turned to the dream I had. A cold chill came over me. I was still confused about the reality of what I felt. Was it all a dream? What if it wasn't? Then what was it? I had so many questions, but I knew that I couldn't tell anyone. People would think I was crazy if I told them what happened to me. There's no such thing as the Boogieman. The Boogieman was a myth created by parents who wanted their children to behave. Here I was, all grown up and wondering if the Boogieman paid me a visit the last two nights. I felt silly.

Since I woke up late, the day seemed to go by quickly. Before I knew it, it was time to start getting ready to go out. I knew Nia would be prompt because she was excited to see Marco that night. I jumped in the shower. Not long, after I heard a knock at my door. I wrapped a robe around me and went to open the door. It was Nia. She cleaned up nicely.

"I can't believe you're not ready!" She said.

"Nia, it's only 8 o'clock. You said we were not leaving until 11 o'clock. I still have three hours," I replied as I laughed sarcastically.

"I know. I'm just nervous," she said as she pushed her way through the door and past me.

She did appear nervous. It was a side of Nia that I had never seen before, but then again, I only met her a couple of weeks ago. I thought about telling her my dreams, but she rushed me to get dressed, so that we could stop somewhere and have a drink before going to the club. She said it would calm her nerves. I knew exactly what she meant. I told her that it would take some time for me to blow dry my hair and straighten it. She said that it was fine and proceeded to my closet to pick out something for me to wear.

As I was flat ironing my hair, I told Nia about NC Kidd and that we agreed to meet at the club. She looked a little confused. She went on about how Marco was going to introduce me to a friend of his. I told her that I would meet him, but I made plans to spend some time with my online interest. She finally gave in and said it was cool, although, she seemed a bit upset about it.

It took me about an hour and a half to get ready. Nia was growing impatient with me. I finally told her let's get out of here. She said, "It's about time. I need that drink already." I laughed and shook my head.

"You crazy girl, but that's why we get along so well," I said, "Yea. I feel ya. I need to calm my nerves as well too."

We walked out of the building and jumped into her car. Nia had a nice vehicle. She was driving a brand new Tahoe. It was fully loaded. Nia's mother could afford it though.

We drove out to some place in the Stone Oak area. We went in, and the place was deserted. Then again, it was barely 10 o'clock. It was really nice--- a bar and grill. They had a huge patio area outside. Nia and I decided to sit out on the patio. The waiter came over. Nia ordered an apple martini, while I ordered cherry vodka sour. He asked for our identification. Nia was only nineteen, but she had a fake ID. I wasn't surprised and I didn't ask any questions since my ID was just as fake as hers.

We sat there and talked for a bit. After two drinks, we decided to leave for the club. We were both quiet on the ride over.

*Nia had the radio on. I think we were both in thought about how
the night might go. Just then, 'The way you are', came on. We both
reached for the volume button. We laughed. We both started sing-
ing. By the time the song was over, we were parking at the Nix
garage. It was the cheapest parking near the club. We would have
to walk a couple of blocks, but that was cool. We would get to walk
by all the other clubs and check out the scenery.*

     *We arrived early enough that we didn't have to stand in
line to go in. We walked in. The place was small, but it had a good
atmosphere. The bar was directly, smack dab in the middle of the
room, so you could order drinks from just about anywhere in the
place. The DJ booth was on the right as you walked in. There were
three VIP areas which weren't too big. We decided to walk around
and check it out. There weren't too many people, but then again
it was still early. It took us all of five minutes to walk around. We
decided to order a drink, cherry vodka sour, and hang out by the
DJ booth.*

     *Before long, people starting strolling in. By midnight,
the place was totally packed. I asked Nia, if she had seen Marco
anywhere. She was looking around, but no luck in spotting him. We
decided to give the place another stroll around to see if we could
find her date. We literally had to push our way through the crowd.
I couldn't believe they allowed that many people in to such a small
area. They had to be breaking some kind of fire code. As we made
our way to the back area, Nia spotted Marco. This huge grin appeared and her face brightened up.*

     *"Hey girl, I gotta go to the restroom," I said, "I'll meet ya
over there in a few minutes, okay?"*

     *"Alright, but hurry the hell up," she said with a laugh.
I turned around to make my way back to the girl's room. I did my*

business, and then checked myself in the mirror on my way out. As I walked out the door, a girl bumped me.

"Watch it bitch!" she said in a loud voice.

"Excuse you; you bumped me," I said to her. Ya better check ya girl," I said to the girl standing next to her.

The girl rolled her eyes at me, turned around, and went into one of the stalls. Her friend said, "Sorry, she's wasted."

"A'ight," I said.

I walked out of the Ladies' room. I was trying to make my way back towards the area that I left Nia at. As I approached the bar, I noticed she and Marco were not there anymore. I looked around, but didn't see them. I laughed and thought to myself, just like Nia. I couldn't help but laugh. I walked up to the bar and asked the bar tender for a cherry vodka sour.

"That one's on me," he said.

I turned around to see who was trying to buy me a drink. I couldn't believe it. It was Maxwell.

"Don't tell me your not gonna accept my offer to buy you that drink?" he said.

I couldn't help but to laugh.

"You know I'm not going to turn a drink down," I said.

"Didn't think so," he replied.

"So, what brings you here tonight freshman?" he said in a sarcastic tone.

"Whatever, there you go with that freshman crap," I said as I grabbed my drink and started to walk off.

He grabbed my hand.

"Hey, hold on, I was only kidding. Can't you take a joke?" he said, "Seriously, I've never seen you here before. What are you doing here tonight?"

"Well, if you must know Maxwell, I'm meeting someone here." I said.

"Oh, I see," he replied.

"Anyone I know," he said with a grin.

"No!" I answered.

"Well, is he here yet?" he asked.

"I don't think so. Uh, I'm not sure," I answered in a hesitant tone.

"A'ight, so why don't you chill with me for a while freshman," he said.

"Why do you insist on calling me freshman?" I asked with an annoyed look on my face.

"Maybe because you have not given me your name freshman," he said with an arrogant laugh.

"Let's start over," he continued, *"Hi, I'm Maxwell and you are?"*

I shook my head and laughed under my breath, but I couldn't hide the smile that appeared on my face.

"I'm Nova. Nice to meet you Maxwell," I replied.

"There, now how bad was that Nova?" he said with a smile.

His smile was gorgeous. I couldn't take my eyes off it or him. We stood there for a good while and just talked. It was that small talk that opposite sexes have when they are interested in one another. It was the "let's get to know each other" type of conversation. In that time, I learned that Maxwell was a year younger than I was, but he was a sophomore. He graduated from high school at the age of seventeen. He was planning on going out for the basketball team this semester. He played for his high school team. Even though he wasn't all-district, he could play the game or so he said.

Before I knew it, it was last call. Maxwell and I learned a lot about each other. I almost forgot that I was there to meet NC Kidd.

"Hey, weren't you suppose to have a date or something?" he asked.

"Oh yea," I laughed.

"Guess you got stood up Angel?" he said.

"His loss," I said, "Wait a minute, what did you say?" He laughed.

"What?" he asked.

"You called me Angel. Nobody, but my friends on MyProfyle knows that name and you're not one of my friends," I said confused.
He continued to smile.

"Don't get mad at me, Nova, but I'm NC Kidd," he said.

"WTF!" I said.

I usually didn't cuss, but I was a little tipsy. I walked off upset with Maxwell.

"Wait," he said as he followed. "Wait Nova! Give me a chance to explain. I tried to tell you at the computer lab, but you didn't give me the time of day. Remember?"

I did remember walking away from him at the lab, but I couldn't help it because he was so annoying that day. It all made sense though. It was the whole reason he even started to talk to me in the lab. Even though, I understood his reasoning, I wasn't going to make it easy for him. He needed to be a little sorry for just a little longer. I remembered I hadn't seen Nia all night, so I started to look around.

"Who are you looking for?" he said.

"I'm getting' punked, right? This is joke on your part and

you're going to introduce me to NC Kidd," I said with a smirk.

"What?" he said, "I told you, Nova, I'm NC Kidd."

"Dang, my luck. I was hoping for someone cuter," I said laughing.

"FYI, I know I look cute tonight," he said with a conceited look on his face.

We both started cracking up. The bartender called last call.

Maxwell offered to walk me back to Nia's car. I was hoping that she didn't leave me. As we walked back to parking garage, we talked. We also laughed. Maxwell was more attractive at the end of the night and it didn't have anything to do with the alcohol. It had everything to do with the conversation that we had, including the messages from MyProfyle, now that I knew he was NC Kidd.

We arrived at Nia's SUV. She wasn't there yet. Maxwell asked if he could kiss me. I laughed, gave him a smile, and politely said, "I don't kiss people I don't know." He tried urging me to go back to his place, which was in the Dominion, but again I turned him down. Just then, Nia came strolling up with Marco.

"Well, you better go," I said.

"A'ight, Imma call you tomorrow," he said.

"Later Maxwell," I replied.

"Good night Nova," he answered.

CHAPTER THREE

I drove up to Nia's mom house. I pulled into the driveway. The lights were on all throughout the house. It was a huge two-story brick home. You could always tell Nia's room apart from the other upstairs' bedrooms by the pink curtains that hung from the window. The living room had a huge picture window. I could see all the girls, Tee, AJ, Luna, Em, Jules, and Rae-Rae. They were standing in the living room. I sat there for a minute. I must have been the last one to arrive.

It felt like yesterday that we had all met at that sorority party during rush week my Freshman year. I couldn't believe that we were in the Fall semester of our junior year. Luna was in Graduate School. Tee and Rae-Rae were getting ready to graduate in the Spring. Tee had been accepted to Med School. Rae-Rae was engaged to marry to her high-school sweetheart. Em, Jules, Nia and I were ready to run the Sorority and the university our senior year. We couldn't wait. We wreaked so much havoc on campus that everyone knew us, and if they didn't it was because they were either a transfer student or in-coming freshman. Either way, it would only be a matter of time before they did know who we were.

I could see the girls talking to each other. Nia's mom was pacing back and forth. I closed my eyes as it took me back to the night that Nia and I got an endless lecture for pulling a disappearing act on everybody. *It was just a year ago. It was the fall semester of our sophomore year. Classes were going to start that*

following Monday, but instead of worrying about buying books
and getting ready, we decided to have a little fun. We jumped in
her Tahoe, not telling a soul, and headed to Corpus. It would be a
weekend get-away on the beach with a little trouble. It was typical
of Nia and me to be spontaneous like that. I was the one always up
to try anything once and I do mean anything. And it was Nia who
always instigated the trouble behind it.

    We had a tank full of gas, a hundred bucks each, no plans
where to stay, but we knew we were going to party, meet new
people, and get some sun. We stopped off at a burger joint to grab
a bite to eat before heading out. As we ate, we talked about the
usual things such as the latest gossip, fashion, and guys. We were
both very much into the online date scene at that point in time.
We finished up and set out for Corpus. We decided to make things
a little more interesting and turned off our cell phones. We both
had different reasons for wanting to get away from it all. I did it
because of the full-blown argument I had with Maxwell and Nia's
reason was because her mom wanted her to transfer to a different
university. However, at the time, I had no idea.

    A short two hours later, we arrived in Corpus Christi, Texas
and headed straight to the beach. We parked at one of the local ho-
tels and walked down to the water. Although, the water wasn't very
clear, the sounds of the waves were so relaxing. I sat down, took off
my flip flops, buried my feet into the hot sand, and closed my eyes.
Paradise was only a dream away. Nia came crashing down next to
me laughing. I opened my eyes and looked at her.

    "What?" I said.

    "Hey chica, see them guys over there?" she asked.

    "Yea, what about 'em?" I answered.

    "Well, they go to Del Mar College and want to know if we

wanna hang out with them," she replied.

"Damn girl, you already met people," I said. "We just got here."

"You know me," she said with a smile.

"Yep, I do and I can smell the trouble you 'bout to get us into," I replied with a smirk.

"C'mon, forget about that jerk," she said, "He probably hasn't even noticed that you're gone or even tried to call you. He's probably with that other chick. You know...the not so pretty one?"

"Ugh, no you didn't. A'ight, what the hell. We're here to have fun, so let's go ova there," I said.

"Now, you're talking and by the way they have plenty of beer," she said.

I stood up and dusted myself off. We walked over to where they camped out. There were six of them sitting around in a circle. They all appeared to be upper classmen. Three of them were Latino, two were African-American and the other was Caucasian. They laughed and seemed to be having a good time. Nia sat down next to one of them.

"This is Paul, Juan, Jose, Mike, James, and Eric" she said. "Uh, Right?"

"Yep, that's right," he said.

He was a very attractive looking guy. He was about 6'2 inches tall, slender, golden light brown skin tone, brown eyes, and a nice smile. He put his hand out to shake mine. I knew right then and there that I was in trouble. He was definitely my type.

"So, you are?" I asked.

"I'm James," he answered.

"Nice to meet you, James" I replied.

He sat back down and told his friend to move over to make room for me. His friend, Eric, just smiled and moved. I sat next to him. They offered us a beer. Neither Nia nor I was going to turn it down. They started to make some small talk by asking us where we were from and what school we went to. Nia had her own little side conversation going on though.

*   "So, what's the University of San Antonio like?" Mike asked.*

*   Mike was cute. He had a deep dark brown skin tone, black eyes, and had an athletic build. He was very clean cut.*

*   "It's a 'ight. There are a lot of students that attend. A lot of parties and the school been 'round for awhile. The campus is huge." I replied.*

*   "Is there a lot to do up there? What's the night life like?" Juan asked.*

*   "Hell yea, there's much to do in SA, Clubs all ov'r the place. Local hot spots are in town, but you can find a club anywhere," I said. "There are also some new and upcoming places on the north and northwest sides of town."*

*   "Cool, we just might have to go check out San Antonio," Jose replied.*

*   Jose and Juan were the Latinos of the group, as was Paul. Jose was about 5'6 inches tall, dark brown hair, brown eyes, and clean-cut. Juan was 5'7 inches tall, black hair, black eyes, and had a shadow among his face as if he had no time for shaving that day. Paul was Nia's type. He was 5'11 inches, light brown skin tone, dark brown wavy hair, clean cut, muscular, and very cute. The white guy, Eric, was about 6 feet 4 inches, very thin, long dirty blonde hair, green eyes, and had a goatee. He was kind of a good-looking guy, but just wasn't my type, but then again, neither were Paul, Juan, or Jose. I was always into a specific type of man.*

We continued to chat and drink. Juan, Eric, and Mike were waiting on their girlfriends to show up. The sun began to set and their girlfriends finally made an appearance.

"Hey, what's up boys? New friends?" she said.
All three of them were Latina, very thin, and very pretty.

"Wat up Baby?" Mike replied, "This is Nova and Nia. They're from San Antonio and just hanging out with us."

"Cool beans," she replied, "Nova and Nia, huh? Well I'm Sabrina, and these are my girls, Tabitha and Kelly."

"Cool beans? What the F... is that?" Nia said loudly.

"Uh, don't mind my home girl. She's had just one too much to drink tonight. Wat up, nice to meet ya'll." I answered before they stepped to Nia.

"Well, now that we arrived, let the party begin. We gonna show ya'll how we do it CC style Nova," Tabitha said.

"I'm down for that," I said with a grin.

Each of them sat down next their guy as if they were making a statement that we should fall back. I just smiled and continued to drink. They had the music going. We were all laughing and having a good time. A Lil' Wayne song came on. Eric reached over to the radio and turned it up. For a minute there I froze, as the thought of Maxwell came upon my mind. It was really crazy as I looked over to my left side and a guy was standing near the water. His features resembled Maxwell so much, but it couldn't be him because he had no idea where I was at. I figured it was just the alcohol playing a crude joke on me. As the song continued to play, I chugged my beer and opened another. Before I knew I had chugged several beers down, as Maxwell kept popping into my mind.

"Hey, are you cool?" James asked.

"Yea, I'm good," I replied.

"How 'bout we go into the water. It might help you sober up some." he said.

"Yea, I think that might be a good idea." I answered.

I stood up with James' help. I had my swimsuit under my clothes, so I took off my shorts and t-shirt, and we headed down to the water. The water was so refreshing. James held me by my waist, so I wouldn't slip and fall. It was kind of nice to be held like that. Maxwell hadn't held me like that in a while and I missed it. We kept walking further out. James knew I wasn't very tall and knew he could go further out than I could. I stopped for a moment as I stood on the tips of my toes.

"C'mon, I'll hold you up," he said, "Don't worry, I won't let you go."

"You better not." I said.

Feeling secure, I put my trust in him---it was those eyes of his that said he wouldn't lie. So, we went out further. He held me in his arms. I probably would have been scared to death had it not been for all the drinks I had. After all, we were in deep water and it was dark out. I could barely see Nia and the others.

"So Nova, is there a guy back in S.A.?" James asked.

"Naw, not anymore." I replied while rolling my eyes.

"Not anymore? What's that all about? If you don't mind me asking?" he asked.

"I did up until this week, but I found out he was seeing someone else. So, I'm single again." I said.

"His loss." he replied.

"Yea, I guess." I answered, "What 'bout you, is there a GF?"

"Nope, no girl." he said as he smiled.

"Cool beans!" I said as I laughed thinking about Nia's

reaction to that expression.

Within a second, James slipped and I slipped out of his arms. I felt the water pushing me down. I was trying to come up for air, but I couldn't swim up. I didn't know which way was up. It was dark all around. I couldn't see anything, including James. I was reaching out for him, but he was nowhere. I started to panic. The water was entering my nose and mouth. I felt a burning sensation in my lungs. I didn't know what it felt like to drown, but this was painful. It felt like I was slipping further and further away. Things started to get darker. For an instance, I saw Maxwell, and then everything went black.

I awoke on the beach. Everybody was standing around me. Nia was crying. She was talking to me, but I couldn't hear anything she was saying. James was standing over me as well.

"What's up?" I said.

"I'm sorry Nova. I didn't mean to let you go." James replied.

"Nia, where's Maxwell?" I asked.

"What are you talking about?" she cried.

"I saw him," I said, "Right before everything turned dark."

"You must have hit your head Nova," she said, "Maxwell isn't here. OMG!! You almost died on us and all you can think about is that jerk. You should be grateful. That man over there saved you. He saw you and James go under, but only saw James come up, so he swam out to help. He pulled you out. You have been out for like ten minutes or so."

"Where?" I said softly, "I wanna thank him."

"Over there," she replied as she pointed, "Where did he go? He was right there a minute ago."

"What did he look like?" I asked.

"Oh, I can see why you thought you saw Maxwell. He did look a little like that a-hole," she said with a little laugh, "You big dummy. Don't ever do that crap again."

"A'ight girl, I'll make an effort not to drown again." I said sarcastically.

We decided that my almost drowning was enough excitement for that weekend. With all that happened, it sobered us both up. We got our things, said our goodbyes to our new friends, and headed back to San Antonio. Of course, Nia got Paul's number and I gave James my number. I told him that he was not to blame and hoped to hear from him.

We drove back to San Antonio. Neither of us said a word. We didn't even listen to the radio. I think we were both grateful that things didn't take a turn for the worst. After all, I could be dead if it wasn't for that Good Samaritan. Within two hours, we drove up to the campus. We parked and headed into the sorority house. We walked into the common area, and there stood Nia's mother and all the girls. She was furious. We got a lecture like no other I had ever had. She started yelling at Nia that this was the reason she wanted her to transfer to another school. She went on about her friends, mainly me, being no good. The girls were angry with us as well...

* * * * * * *

I felt something pinning me down. I was fighting to open my eyes. I couldn't open them, but I heard it. The same growl I have heard time and time again. I was screaming, "Please stop, please!!" I felt a sharp pain rip across my chest. A voice whispered, "You're mine, Nova." A loud banging noise startled me. The growl stopped and my eyes opened slowly. I could barely focus them.

"Nova, Nova, wake up," AJ said. "What are you doing?"

I looked over and AJ was banging on my car window. I looked at Nia's house and all the girls were standing at the window.

"Are you okay, Nova?" she asked.

I took off my seat belt and opened my car door. I reassured AJ that I was fine and just dozed off thinking about Nia.

"Well, come inside. The cops will be here any minute," she said.

"Yeah, okay," I said as I was trying to wake up and shake off the images of another nightmare.

We walked up to the house and into the living room. I hugged all my sorority sisters and Nia's mom. I sat down on the couch. I was still stunned from the incident in the car, but put it off to the back of my head. Before long, the San Antonio police showed up. Mrs. Carmichael opened the door for the officers. Panicked, but she kept calm, so she could explain that Nia was missing. The officers took down the information Nia's mom provided. They began to talk to us about the incident and asked if any of us knew where she might have gone before her disappearance. I looked at AJ and nodded for her to come over my way.

"What's up Nova?" she asked.

"We need to tell 'em...'bout her date with that online guy," I said. "I think Nia will understand."

She nodded her head in agreement and walked toward T and Jules. She took them aside. They turned to me and each gave a nod of approval. AJ then walked up to Em and whispered to her. Em gave the nod as well. Luna and Rae-Rae were talking with the officers, so AJ waited for them to finish before going over to them. The officers proceeded to talk with Tee and Jules. AJ pulled both

Luna and Rae-Rae aside, and spoke with them. Rae-Rae turned to me and nodded. Luna looked in my direction, then looked at AJ, and shook her head as to say no way. AJ turned and looked at Luna in disbelief. Luna gave a nod voting against saying anything to anybody. Although, I was shocked, I wasn't surprised. Luna kept to oath of sister hood. She knew it would be a betrayal even though Nia may actually be in danger. I walked over to Luna.

"We got to do this for Nia," I said to her. "She may be in some real trouble."

"You know how I feel about this. Nia wouldn't want us to tell her mom about her private life. We can figure this out amongst us." She said.

"Sorry Luna, I know you out rank me and the others, but I've been given the go ahead by everybody else, so we out vote you." I replied.

"Watch it Nova. You're over stepping your boundaries," she answered. "I'm going to let this one go. Make the call. It's on you now."

The girls were focused on Luna and me and the intense discussion that was obviously taking place. One of the officers walked up to us.

"Is there a problem here ladies?" he asked.

"No, officer, but I believe I have some information that could help." I said. I proceeded to tell the officer about the online date that Nia had arranged. The officer asked if I or any of the girls had any details about the young man that Nia had met online.

"Do you know his name, address, user ID, or anything else that may help?" he asked.

"No, I didn't get to talk to her yesterday. She was trying to tell me about the guy, but I was late for class and told her I would meet up with her later. Later never came." I answered as a state of guilt overcame me.

I looked at Nia's mom. She was crying. I walked over to her and apologized for not telling her sooner. I tried to explain to her my reasoning, but she was upset and asked me to leave her home.

"Leave Nova, leave now!" she cried out.

"I'm very sorry Mrs. Carmichael. I didn't mean to hurt you." I said. Mrs. Carmichael wasn't much of a fan of mine. She actually told Nia from the day she met me that she didn't like me. I think that made Nia want to be my friend all the more.   I walked out of the home and Tee came out after me.

"She doesn't mean it Nova. She's hurting." She said.

"It's all good. I would hate me too. In fact, I do for not being a better friend." I yelled out.

"Go back to the sorority house Nova. We will be right behind you." Tee replied.

I got into my car and drove off. How could I not have known about this mystery guy that Nia met online? We were tight. I knew about every guy she dated since freshman year. Yet, I knew not one thing about this one. Why? Was I caught up to much into my own thing with Maxwell? I didn't know what I was going to do, but I wasn't going to let it go.

I drove back to the sorority house. I walked in and went straight up to our room. I sat on her bed and looked around. I found myself staring at the computer. Of course, there has to be some trail left. All I had to do was log onto my accounts and search her profiles. Look for new friends she just added and try to narrow it down to who she may have been talking to. I walked over to the computer. I sat down. I turned the computer on. A picture we had taken together at a party was on the screen saver. A smile came over me, but I was still sad. I heard the girls enter the common area downstairs.

"Nova, where you at?" AJ called out.

"Up stairs, in my room." I yelled back to her.

They came upstairs. They were all standing there.

"What are you doing on the computer? This is not the time for chatting online. Nia's missing." Rae-Rae said.

"Really, duh? I know. I started to think of a way to find out who Nia's mystery date was. And it hit me. Log on to my accounts and search her profile for new friends added in the past month." I replied.

"And then what Nova? Ask them if they had anything to do with Nia being missing. I'm sure one of them will say they are responsible." Luna said sarcastically.

"No, but if we can narrow it down, and talk to them. You know how people online seem to tell you more than they should. How many new friends could Nia have made in the last two or three weeks? Think about it." I said.

"No, wait Luna. She may have something. We can do this. Damn, look at us. We're all smart, beautiful and persuasive." Jules replied.

"You have a point, but this guy has to know what we look like if he has been in Nia's profile. We are all on her top friend's list. How are we gonna pull off that?" Rae-Rae asked.

"He's not gonna meet one of us. He's gonna meet someone that doesn't exist. We're gonna create a profile. It doesn't have to have a picture. How many people do you come across with no pics?" I replied.

"That may work and what do we do when it comes time to

meet these men smarty or if they ask for a picture?" Luna asked.

"I don't know that right now, but it's a start and the only plan that seems capable of finding our sister. Besides if someone asks for a pic, then we send one, any pic, not like they gonna know. All I know is that we need to find our girl." I said as I looked at Luna.

"Fine, let's do it. Besides the seven of us have a better chance of finding her than the police. We got this online thing, so let's create our profile." Luna replied.

We sat around the computer and started creating profiles on MyProfyle, YourIt, and Friendbook. It took us some time that night because we has disagreements about what things we should write under interests, background layouts, and music. We wanted to create the whole illusion of real profiles and not take a chance of someone realizing it was bogus. By sunrise, all three profiles were created and all we had to do was to narrow down anyone that Nia might have been interested in or met within the last couple of weeks.

CHAPTER FOUR

As Nia and Marco walked up to her SUV, she yelled, "where you been all night girl? We were looking for you in the club." Nia wasn't drunk, but she was having fun and appeared to be in a very good mood.

"I was enjoyin' some time with a new friend."

She giggled and nodded her head at me as if she was approving. I jumped into the passenger side of her SUV. She and Marco were behind the vehicle. They were looking at each other like neither of them wanted to say good night. I watched from the rear view mirror. As Marco leaned in to kiss her, I pushed the horn and Nia started laughing. Marco didn't seem amused, but Nia couldn't help but smile. They said goodnight and she walked over to the driver side and got into the vehicle.

"Girl, you're so wrong," Nia said as she giggled. "He was gonna kiss me".

"I know, but now he'll wanna kiss you even more. Believe me, he's already thinking 'bout you," I said as I winked.

"Do you think so?" she said hesitantly.

"Please girl, that boy has it bad for you. He don't even realize how much trouble he's in with ya."

"Yeah, you're right!" She yelled out over the loud music I turned up while she was talking.

The volume on the radio was all the way up, but anyone could tell that neither Nia nor I was listening to it. We both were in *deep thought. Before we knew it, we had arrived at the dorm and both heading inside and up to our rooms. We were laughing and joking around about who would actually get that first kiss from our certain admirers. Nia pushed me out the way.*

"It would have been me if you had not interrupted."
I laughed and she told me that I owed her one for that.

"It's all good." I said. "For all you know, he's probably not even that great of a kisser." I couldn't help but laugh. Nia stopped laughing and I put in my two cents.

"Well, for your sake you better hope I find out soon or else."

"Or else what, shut up girl? Ain't nobody scared of you."
"I know, but I thought it was funny."
"Yeah, yeah, whatev'r girl." I rolled my eyes at her.
"Hey Nova, you didn't tell me about NC Kidd" Nia said.
"Oh yea, long story girl and I'm tired, but, I'll hit ya up tomorrow."

"Oh hell no, you're not keeping me in suspense. Besides I won't be able to sleep," she said as she stood there with her hands on her hips.

"Ugh! Let me change and I'll come ov'r to your room and tell ya 'bout it."

"Alright, but hurry the hell up," she said.
"Whatev'r, give me a minute." I walked into my room.

The room was dark, but the glare from the street light was visible from the window. I looked over to my roommate's bed, but she was not there. I found it strange because it was three o'clock in the morning. She was always in bed by 11:00 p.m. As I walked in, I heard a sound. It came from my side of the room by my bed. I turned over to look where the noise was coming from, but didn't see anything. Suddenly, I felt a chill run up my back, as something passed right by me. It felt as if someone's hand had touched my face. My first reaction was to pull away from whatever it was and then I reached for the light.

As the light came on, I didn't see anything or anybody in the room. There was nothing in sight. I thought it was probably my imagination playing tricks on me or that I had too many drinks at the club. Either way, I didn't want to go to sleep in my room. I went to my dresser and pulled out a pair of shorts and t-shirt. I changed right there and grab my keys and headed out the door to Nia's room. I turned off the light. As I looked toward my bed, I saw these red eyes looking my way. I stared at them for a minute, but then closed my eyes quickly as if I opened them back up, it would be gone. I opened my eyes. I saw those red eyes looking back at me. I slammed the door shut and ran to Nia's room.

I banged on Nia's door. She was laughing as she opened it up. She looked at me and stopped laughing.

"What's wrong Nova?" she asked.
I didn't say anything because I couldn't say anything.

"Okay, ignore me then, but get your butt in here and tell me about NC Kidd," she said. "Nova, seriously, what's wrong?"

"I don't know Nia, but I think my mind is playin' tricks on me."

"Girl, you probably drank too much tonight," she said as she smiled. "Get in here!"

"Would it be cool if I crashed here tonight Nia?"

"Whatever girl, it's cool since I don't have a roommate," she said. "Now tell me about your date."

I sat on the bed across from Nia's and started telling her about NC Kidd and Maxwell being the same person. But like Nia, my story about Maxwell was interrupted by her telling me about her night with Marco. It was the first time I really understood that Nia was about the world revolving around Nia. I didn't mind though because I didn't have to go back to my room and face what I thought I had seen. I laid down and listen to Nia's story about her night at the club. I closed my eyes and soon drifted off to my dreams. My dreams were racing back and forth that night. I was trying to make sense of them all.

The only one I could make out was about a guy I didn't even know. He was a very attractive black man. He had a great smile that showed his dimples off. His eyes were light brown and something caught my attention in them. He was saying something to me, but I couldn't hear him. It seemed important, so I was trying to walk closer to him, but the closer I tried to get to him, the farther away he became. I tried to reach for him, and he put out his hands, but I couldn't grab on. I starting walking faster towards him as I was asking what was he trying to tell me. He kept talking to me, but I just couldn't hear him. Then a loud sound woke me up. It was my cell phone.

I opened my eyes and reached over to it. I picked it up. It was Maxwell. As promised, he was calling.

"Will you answer that damn thing," Nia shouted, as she seemed annoyed by the ringer playing on my phone. I had forgotten that I was in her room.

"Hello."

It was the first time that I heard Maxwell's voice on the phone and it was very seductive. He asked how I was doing. I told him that I was still in bed, but everything was good. I couldn't help but put a smile on my face as he spoke to me. We chatted for a little while. It was just the normal talk about having a good time with each other the night before.

My dream about the good-looking guy seemed to fade away at that point. Maxwell asked me if we could go out that night. He invited me to a movie. I hesitated for a minute before accepting his invitation. He went on to let me know which movie theater, what movie and time before we said our see you later. As I hung up the phone, Nia popped up beside me and with a giggle.

"I guess that Maxwell boy likes you, huh?" I laughed right along with her.

I got up and told Nia I would see her later. She said alright, and headed back to her bed to lay back down. I opened the door and looked back at Nia.
"Hey girl, thanks for lettin' me crash here last night."

I closed her door and walked over to my room. As I put the key in to open the door, a flash of those red eyes looking at me came to my mind. My hand started to shake, but it was daylight out, so I knew I had nothing to worry about. I opened the door and there stood my roommate.
"Hey, is everything good 'cause I didn't see you last night when I got in?" I asked her. She just looked at me.
"Sorry, I didn't mean to scare you or anything, but I stayed at a friend's house last night.

I looked at her with some doubt about her explanation because I had never seen her with anyone since we became room-mates, but that was her life and none of my business.

"Oh, a'ight girl, that's cool."

I walked over to my bed and sat down. I was thinking about what I was going to wear for my date with Maxwell.

"Nova," my roommate said. "I just wanted to let you know that I will probably be out of town next weekend, so the room will

be all yours."

"Oh, okay," I replied. "I know it's none of my business Lilly, but you sure everything is a'ight?"

"Yes Nova, I'm just going away on a weekend retreat with an organization I'm involved with," she replied.

"Sounds cool, I guess. Have fun then," I answered her.

She picked up her books and walked out of the room. I laid down on my bed and looked up at the ceiling. I started to remember my dream. It was weird because I had no idea who the guy was that I was dreaming about, but somehow he captured my attention. Just as my mind started to drift off, I knew I had to get up and take a shower. I walked over to the closet and pulled out a pair of jeans and a shirt. I headed to the bathroom for a long hot shower.

I got dressed and decided to take a walk over to the lab, so I could get online. I decided to take the scenic route again. It was a beautiful day out, but it was hot. I arrived at the lab and proceeded to walk in and log on to one of the computers. I went on to My-Profyle. To my surprise, Maxwell was online. He sent me a message asking what I was doing. I replied telling him I was talking to several of my fans. He sent another message just with the letters... LOL. I replied and told him that I would see him later that night at the movie theater. I logged off the site and logged onto Friendbook. No one was really on, but then again it was a Sunday afternoon. After a couple of hours of logging on to Friendbook and YourIt, I soon got bored and decided to call it an afternoon and head back to my dorm.

I walked out of the building and looked around. The campus was deserted. I saw some students hanging out over by the sombrilla area. I started to walk over toward them, but knew I had to get back to get ready for my date with Maxwell. As I turned

*in the opposite direction, I bumped into a fascinating character,
although I didn't know it just yet.*

*"Oops! I'm sorry, my bad," I said as I smiled at him.
He was about six feet tall, very nicely dressed, and attractive.*

*"It's all good," he replied. "No big deal."
His voice was very charming as was his smile.*

*"So what's your name Smooth," he asked.
I giggled, which I rarely do.*

"It's Nova."

"Cool name, Smooth," he said.

"And you are?" I asked.

"It's Duane, but call me whatever you like," he said.

"Play'r... I see how it is," I replied with a laugh.

*"Now, why you gonna label me like that and not even know
me, Smooth," he replied with a smirk.*

*"Probably for the same reason you labeled me," I said
sarcastically while laughing. He laughed back.*

*"You a'ight. I ain't never seen you 'round campus, so what
year are you?"*

"It's my freshman year."

"Cool Smooth, welcome to college life," he said.

"What year are you?"

*"This is my last year and lucky me, I got to meet you," he
said with a smile.*

*"Hmmm...true dat," I replied., "Well, nice meeting you.
Maybe we'll run into each other again, but I gotta get back to my
dorm. See ya 'round player."*

*"Oh, you can count on it, Smooth," he replied. "I don't
know, but I have a feeling that you and I are gonna be good friends
some day."*

I walked off and didn't look back, but heard him laughing and knew he was watching me as I left. I finally arrived back at the dorm and went up to my room to get ready for the movie date. I walked into my room and over to my bed. I turned on my flat iron and then sat down on my bed for a minute. I started to get a little nervous about the date thing. Even though I had fun with Maxwell at the club, it really wasn't an official date. This would actually be the first time we were going out. My mind started to wonder, like it always does when I like someone. Next thing I know, an hour had passed and I needed to hurry and get ready to meet Maxwell at the theater.

After I did my hair and was getting dressed, my phone rang. I knew it was Nia because I had given her number a unique ring tone. I shook my head because I knew she was in her room and instead of walking two doors down and coming over to talk, she was calling. I answered.

"Hey girl, you almost ready for your date?"

"Yeah, wat up?"

"How are you getting there?"

I laughed and replied, "Funny thing, I hadn't thought 'bout that yet."

"Yeah, I figured that," she said as she laughed, "Well, I could lend you my SUV if you want."

"Naw girl, I ain't trying to do all that. I don't wanna borrow your vehicle."

"Well, how about if I give you a ride because I really do need to go run some errands right quick."

I knew Nia didn't need to run any errands. Nia was curious about Maxwell and she insisted that she give me a ride. I couldn't turn her down even if I wanted to because she would have kept on and on until I agreed.

"*A'ight girl. Thanks, cool of you,*" *I said.* "*I'm almost ready. I'll head ov'r to your room in a couple of minutes.*"

"*Cool, alright I'll wait for you then,*" *she replied as she hung up the phone.*

I checked myself in the mirror. I smiled as I slowly turned to look the outfit over. I laughed and shook my head as I turned for the door and made my way down to Nia's room.

I knocked. Nia opened the door. "*Well, come on. You're going to be late for this date with Mr... Uh, what's Maxwell last name anyways?*" *she asked.*

"*Uh, I don't know yet,*" *I answered, thinking to myself that I didn't know a whole lot about Maxwell.*

"*I guess that's one question I should ask tonight.*"

"*Yes ma'am, that sure is one you need to know,*" *she said.* "*Didn't your mom ever tell you that you shouldn't go out with strangers?*"

I laughed.

"*Yeah, she did. But this is the cutest stranger I ever met.*"

We both laughed about it and walked down the hall of the dorm and out to her SUV. I started to really feel nervous about going to meet Maxwell. I think Nia realized it because she starting babbling about Marco. She was trying to get my mind off the date. She accomplished it. The ride seemed to take forever, but we finally arrived at the movie theater. Maxwell was standing in the front of the theater. I smiled and told Nia that was him. She looked at him, then looked at me.

"*I can't really see him from this distance, but nice I guess.*"

I couldn't help but laugh.

"*So, are you going to need me to pick you up?*"

"*I'm not sure, but I will text you if I do need a ride back. a'ight,*"

"*Okay girl, have fun!*" she said.

I got out of her SUV and walked toward the front of the movie theater and over to Maxwell. He looked at me and said, "*Cute.*"

"*Whatev'r,*" I replied.

"*I was talking about me,*" he said, "*cause you know I look cute tonight.*" I laughed at his joke and we went inside. He had already purchased the movie tickets. We walked into the theater. It was dark and nearly empty. There were only a few people waiting on the movie to start. We walked up towards the back of the theater. He led the way and walked into the second to the last isle. We sat down. As I tried to get comfortable, he pulled up the armrest between us and pulled me over toward him. I looked at him puzzling and he laughed.

"*Don't worry, I'm not gonna bite you or anything,*" he said. I smiled. I felt at ease sitting in that movie theater with Maxwell and no longer felt those butterflies in my stomach. Even though I just met him, it felt like I knew him for such a long time. It was a strange but good feeling. Maxwell asked if I was ok as he got a little closer to me. I felt his hand on my arm as he slid it down to hold my hand. I told him yes looking into his eyes. He smiled as he turned his head away and toward the screen to watch the movie. We didn't say much after that, but nothing more really needed to be said in that moment, as we held each other's hand.

As the credits rolled, he leaned over to me and said, "*Guess you'll be coming over to my place for dinner?*"

"*What makes you think that I'm gonna go to your place Mr....Umm, what is your last name Maxwell?*" I asked.

"It's Brenan".

"Okay, Mr. Brenan, what makes you think I will go back to your place for dinner?"

"Because dinner has already been prepared for us and is going to get cold if we don't leave now and stop this chit-chatting."

"Well, I'm just curious as to how you assumed I would be having dinner with you?" I said looking at him while raising my right eyebrow.

"Oh, I knew you wouldn't refuse me Nova Marie Salinas," he answered.

"What? How in the world did you find out my full name?"

"You know, there is this amazing little thing called the internet and you can search out for all sorts of information on people," he said while laughing. "Actually Nova, you should be more careful about what you post on MyProfyle."

"Very funny, but I see your point. So, I guess I will have dinner with you tonight," I replied feeling a bit silly.

We got up and started to make our way out of the movie theater. We walked out the front doors and Maxwell told me to wait there while he went to get his car. It took him all of two minutes to pull up to me in a brand new white M6 BMW convertible. I don't know why I wasn't shocked that he owned such a nice car, after all he was only a nineteen-year-old college student. I guess I would have been, if I had known that his car was worth a little over of a hundred grand, but seeing all the nice cars parked on campus in the student parking lots made me not give it a second thought. He put his car in park and got out. He walked around the backside and came over to open the passenger door. I think I was more im- pressed by that than what he was driving.

"Nice car." He laughed and nodded at me.

"Yea, it was a birthday gift."

I got in as he closed the door behind me. He proceeded to walk back over to the driver side and got in. He smiled, reached over for my seat belt, and fastened it.

"As long as I'm around, you won't have to worry 'bout anything happening to you." He shifted the gear and off we went down Loop 1604 and up IH-10 to the Dominion.

It took Maxwell about twenty minutes to get us to his home. We turned into the Dominion, which is one of the wealthiest sub-divisions in San Antonio, Texas. NBA players and coaches, doctors, attorneys, even singers, and movie stars called it home. I had never been through the sub-division before. I only passed it by several times on my way to a Havana club down the street. I once dreamed of living in a huge mansion. I had no idea that one day I would actually be dinning in one of those homes. Maxwell turned onto a long road that led us up to his home secured behind a huge black-iron gate and security station. As we pulled up to the security station, the security guard opened the gate and waved us through. I smiled at Maxwell.

"Is all the security really necessary just for you? Who the heck are you?" Maxwell laughed but not at the questions, rather at the look on my face, as I stared in amazement at his home or I should say mansion.

He parked the BMW directly in front of the home. As I got out, I noticed that his home sat on top of a hill and on about two and a half acres of land. It was an incredible sight, and the view over looking San Antonio was so beautiful. The mansion was something out of a storybook. I had never seen a home quite like it. It looked like a palace. Maxwell told me that his parents had it built in the summer of 2000 when they moved to San Antonio. He said the architect put a Mediterranean influence on the place. I didn't know anything about architecture, but I knew that his home had to be worth several million dollars. We walked up to the front door and he opened it and led me inside. I was a little shocked that his front door was not even locked, but I guess with that much security there was no reason to lock his home. As we walked in, my facial expression must have told him that I had never been in such a beautiful home.

"Welcome to my home Nova. Let me show you around."

The first thing I noticed was the dual serpentine-like staircases that led to the upper level of the mansion. Each of the staircases led to its own wing. In between the staircases hung a huge brass chandelier, that hung down in front of the hand carved marble fireplace. The staircase on the left lead up to the east wing, while the staircase on the right lead up the west wing. The floor throughout the home was made of marble. Each wing had four bedrooms and four bathrooms.

Each wing had its own master bedroom with a hand carved marble fireplace in it as well. The downstairs consisted of the kitchen, two living areas, two dining areas, a media room, a wine cellar, and three more bathrooms. Maxwell told me that his mother decorated the rooms and which all contained Italian furnishings. He led me outside to the back. Outside was an entirely different view, but just as beautiful. There was a huge pool, Jacuzzi, a bar, and a full size basketball court. His home was so unrealistic to me, and it seemed like I was in my dream.

Maxwell looked at me and said, "Well, this is our little home away from home."

"What do you mean by little?"

With a laugh, he said, "It's only about 12,000 square feet."

"Oh, is that all."

"Yes, our home in North Carolina is probably twice as big, but enough talk about my home because I do believe it's time for dinner."

"Well, I do believe that I'm your guest, so please lead the way. I wouldn't want to get lost in this place."

"Very funny Nova, but I hope that you enjoy dinner. I hope you don't mind, but I usually eat in the kitchen instead of the dining area," he said with a smile.

"No, actually I don't mind. I usually don't eat in either of my dining areas as well," I said sarcastically.

Maxwell laughed and we proceeded to walk to the kitchen. I stood in the kitchen surrounded by stainless steel appliances and Italian wood cabinetry. In the middle of the kitchen was an island, and the countertop was made of marble. The barstools were hand-carved of Italian wood as well. Someone prepared the food and placed it on the island for us. I didn't see anyone else in the home. I saw no maids or butlers anywhere in sight. I smiled as I looked at the meal. It was a burger and fries. I was curious as to what the meal would be after seeing the car and the home. In fact, I was starting to wonder if Maxwell was your normal college student. The meal and his smile put my mind at ease.

"Uh, you do like burgers and fries, right?"

"Yes, I guess I'm your typical burger and fries girl."

"Oh no Nova, you are anything but typical."

"If you say so Maxwell, can we just eat already?"

"Of course, anything you like."

We sat down and started to eat while we talked. I asked Maxwell about North Carolina because he mentioned his parents had another home there. I found out that Maxwell was born in

North Carolina and moved to San Antonio with his parents for business purposes. He decided to stay in S.A. to attend college when his parents returned to his hometown two years ago. Maxwell was home schooled most of his education. However, his parents decided to send him to public school for his high school years. He told me he was an average student that kept his grades up, so he could play high school basketball. I think he was being modest because Maxwell seemed to be very intelligent.

We continued to talk and I continued to listen and learn more about him. I didn't finish the entire meal, I was more interested in Maxwell, but it probably was the best burger that I had ever tasted. We decided to move our conversation to one of the living areas. Like all the other rooms, it too had Italian decor. We sat down on one of the sofas.

"So Nova, now that you know a little more about me, will you consider hanging out with me again sometime soon?"

"Well, I guess you a'ight, so I'll consider it," I said as I smiled at him.

"I'm being serious Ms. Salinas. I'm asking you out again."

"I don't get it Maxwell. Why me? I'm mean, I'm looking around at how you live and I figure you could probably have any girl on campus you want, so why me?"

He smiled at me and winked.

"You really don't know why? C'mon, look at you, that light brown complexion, those big brown eyes, your light brown hair, gorgeous smile, great sense of humor, you have a confidence about yourself, but you don't let it go to your head, you're very smart and beautiful. You got it going on Nova. Don't take this wrong, nobody's perfect, but you're pretty much damn near it."

I was embarrassed to hear Maxwell say all those things

about me. I think he knew that when I looked down and away from him. He placed his hand under my chin and pulled my head back up, so I was looking at him again, and leaned in to kiss me for the first time. All those butterflies that left at the movie theater suddenly were in my stomach again. There was something amazing about that kiss. I felt a shock throughout my body. I don't know what it feels like to be struck by lightning, but that's the only way I can describe it. I opened my eyes to look at him.

"So, what do you mean nearly perfect?"

"You are a bit short, Nova, being only 5'3", but I can over look that cause you are cute."

"I see Maxwell. And as you said, nobody's perfect. Let's just say, you're not quite as tall as I like them either," I said as I winked at him.

We both smiled, and continued to talk. I didn't kiss Maxwell again that night, but that one kiss would be a memory that would last me a lifetime. I agreed to see Maxwell again before I left and he took me home that night. The ride home was refreshing as we drove down Loop 1604, back to campus, with the top down on his BMW convertible. Maxwell held my hand the entire time. It was a perfect ending to a perfect night.

CHAPTER FIVE

As the sun made its way through the window of the room that Nia and I had shared for the past year and a half, the girls were exhausted from a long night of creating the online profiles and decided to get some sleep. I, on the other hand, couldn't sleep and wanted to start searching for any people that Nia added to her friend's list within the last three or four weeks.

"Hey Nova, get some rest," AJ said. "You've been at the computer all night". I looked at AJ and she knew that I wouldn't be able to sleep, so she nodded her head and closed the door behind her as she left.

As always, time flies by when you're preoccupied on things that matter. All my sisters were sound asleep, but I was on a mission to find my girl who was M.I.A. My search started on MyProfyle.com because it was the social network that we all most often used. I knew it would be the one profile that Nia had more friends on than any of the others. I just didn't really know how busy the girl was making friends on the site.

I proceeded to her friend's list and searched for all new friends she made in the last month. Nia had over four hundred friends, but she had only added about thirty new friends lately. As I looked through the new people she added, I noticed several guys that were on my friend's list as well. Some had recently made contact with me while others hadn't yet, but I added them anyways. In all, I saw only about fifteen screen names that I did not recognize. In my search, one name jumped out from the screen at me. I couldn't believe it, but it was someone who made contact with me through a message a couple of weeks prior. I couldn't forget his screen name because the message he sent me was very interesting, so much so, that it caught my attention.

His user name was Brakcz. He introduced himself in his message. He said he lived in Europe. He was a music artist, but owned his own shop. He was twenty-something. Music was his first love, but he explained that he was looking for his soul mate. He said even though he was only in his twenties, he felt like he had spent a life time searching for someone to complete him. He spoke several languages, including English, Spanish, French, and Dutch. He attached a picture of himself. He was very handsome. He had a deep dark chocolate skin complexion. He was very well dressed in dark blue suit. He had dark black eyes and an alluring smile. I couldn't tell how tall he was in the photo, but he did have a slender build.

I was very interested in his message and wanted to reply immediately, but I didn't want to seem too eager, so I put it off. With everything that had been going on with Maxwell and me, I just hadn't found the time to get back to him. And now, with the issue of Nia being missing, well, Brackz being on her friend's list could be a bad thing. I continued to write down all the user names that were new to Nia's friend list. As soon as I jotted them all down, I decided to log onto the next site, YourIt.com.

I logged on to my account and scrolled down to my top friend's list, and clicked on Nia's pic. The screen took me to her page. I clicked on all friends, and did a search for any new friends added. Nia had only made about seven new friends on this site. However, I noticed that three of those were the same users from

MyProfyle.com, including Brackz. I realized this definitely was not good. As before, I jotted down the screen names and put an asterisk mark next to DatBoi, Brakcz, and PrtiBoi. I exited out of YourIt. com and logged onto Friendbook.com.

I didn't think I would find anyone on Nia's page that I didn't know on the site, as this was a site for friends. We all used this site for contact only with our real friends. Even though I didn't think I would find anyone I didn't know, I still clicked on Nia's page from my friend's list and scrolled down for her friend's list. I clicked on her friends and I was startled but what popped onto my screen. There were two faces that I did not recognize and one that I did, but didn't expect to see. I wrote down the two user names that I didn't recognize. And then, I stopped to look at the face that startled me. It was Maxwell.

I really didn't know what to make of Maxwell being on Nia's page. Not only did it feel like someone had slapped me into next week, but my mind was racing with so many questions. How could I have not known that Nia was talking to Maxwell, or why did I not notice he was on her friend's list before? Maybe it was because I never went into her friend's list before this because I had no reason to. The only time I ever looked at someone on her page was when she asked me to, so I could give her my opinion about that person. Regardless, I didn't understand it because Nia hated Maxwell and vice versa. But, none-the-less, there he was on her page.

I continued to stare at his picture, and then I felt a sharp pain creep up on me. My head was pounding and I didn't know if it was from the lack of sleep or all the thoughts racing through my brain. I put my head down, but my eyes did not turn away from the screen or Maxwell. A flashback appeared, as my eyes grew too heavy to keep them open any longer.

I soon recalled the first time that Nia met Maxwell, well, almost met him. We went to the mall. I had seen a pair of shoes online and wanted to see if they had my size at the Guess store. So, AJ, Nia, and I decide to drive over and do some shopping. We parked on the second level of the garage by Macy's, as we always did. We got out of the car and were laughing, and talking about nothing in particular. We walked into the mall. Nia was on the left, AJ in the middle, and I was on the right as we passed Macy's. I was talking to AJ and glanced over at a guy coming up the stairs, but could only see his back side. I didn't give it much attention and kept talking to AJ. He passed me by, and I remember thinking in that one quick moment, as he passed, that he smelled really good. I didn't look at him though because Nia jumped into the conversation.

We made our way to the Guess store and started looking around. Nia and AJ went in their own direction, and I headed straight for the shoes. I immediately saw the shoes I wanted and started looking around for a sales person when my text ring tone went off. I took my phone out of my back pocket. It was Maxwell.

His text said that a funny thing just happened. I replied to ask what it was. He instantly replied, letting me know that he just passed me by. I turned to look around the store, but he was nowhere in sight. I thought he was joking with me. So, I text back that he was funny, but since I didn't see him around, it was impossible that he just passed me by. As I was texting, Nia came over to me.

"Who are you texting girl?"

"Maxwell. He said he just passed me by, but I don't see him in the store."

Nia started to look around the store. She had been very curious to find out what Maxwell looked like in person since that day that he and I went on that movie date.

Just then, my text went off again. He explained that he was going up the stairs by Macy's and passed me by. I laughed. Nia looked at me and said, "Well, what did he say?"

"Did you see that guy that passed us by when we turned the corner at Macy's?"

"Yes, that black guy with the dreads?"

"Yea, that was him. That was Maxwell."

"Well, why didn't he stop you or say hi?"

AJ came over.

"What's goin' on?"

As I was going to tell AJ, Nia jumped in and started telling her that Maxwell passed us by and didn't even say anything.

"Was he that guy that came up the stairs Nova?"

"Yeah, that was him."

"Yeah, I thought I recognized him from somewhere, but couldn't place him. You showed us a pic of him, but it wasn't clear on his profile."

"Ugh, the point is that he didn't even say anything to her AJ. I mean he could have stopped her and not texted her to let her know he saw her. What, is he still in high school or something?"

"Well, let me ask 'em girl."

I knew I had no right to question Maxwell about not stopping me, but Nia wasn't going to let up with the whole situation. I texted him back and asked him why he didn't stop me because I would have said hi and introduced him to my friends. Maxwell took a couple of minutes to reply, but he said he didn't want to interrupt my conversation. He said I looked caught up talking to my girls and didn't want to be rude.

I smiled and turned to Nia and AJ and told them what his response was. Nia immediately rolled her eyes. She went on about how he seemed to be avoiding me altogether, because she saw him turning to look in the opposite direction to avoid me seeing him. I looked at AJ and asked her if she saw that as well. AJ looked at me, then looked at Nia and told her that she didn't see him do that. I just laughed it off and said, "Oh well, doesn't really matter at this point."

AJ and Nia wanted to go to Agaci, which was a clothing store across from Guess. I told them that I would be there in a bit, but first, I needed to get the shoes I wanted. As I asked the sales person for my size, I remembered that I didn't reply to Maxwell. So, I texted back letting him know that I was with my girls, Nia and AJ. He replied that he knew that because he saw me with a black girl and a white girl, but that really didn't matter because he wanted to know when we were going to see each other again. I replied and told him that he just saw me again, but on the real I would let him know later because I had to go find my girls before they left me at the mall.

The sales person came out with the shoes. I took them up to the counter, made my purchase, and then walked over to Agaci. I found Nia still discussing the topic of Maxwell. AJ just looked at me with her eyes wide as to say oh my gosh, she won't shut up about it.

"Wat up Nia? What's wrong?"

"That boy is what's wrong Nova. I just think he's all wrong for you."

"Why?"

"I don't like him or the way he acted towards you. It was so wrong."

"Well, I know you my girl, but that's on me. Nia, if he wanted to avoid me, then why would he text me? He didn't have to let me know he passed me by."

"I don't know, maybe he's playing some kind of game."
I rolled my eyes and Nia got upset. She started getting louder. A sales person came over and tapped me on the shoulder.

"Excuse me," she said.
I didn't pay attention to her.

"Excuse me," she said again.

"Nova!"

Just then, I felt a stinging sensation rip across my upper back and left shoulder.

"NOVA!" I heard with a snarl, as I felt a stream of hot air roll over my ear and onto my face. My eyes opened. I was on the floor and my chair was knocked over. The pain was excruciating. AJ ran into my room.

"Nova, what happened? Are you okay?"
I looked at her and didn't say anything.

"OMG! What happened to you? How did you cut your back Nova? You're bleeding."

"What?"

"Look in the mirror."

I got up, and went over to the mirror and turned around to see two huge slash marks across my back and shoulder. I wasn't sure who or what it was, but something had ripped into my shirt and cut in to my skin deep enough to cause blood to drip from the wounds.

AJ looked scared, but she ran out to get the first aid kit. She yelled for Tee to come help since she was the pre-med student. Tee came running into the room and asked what happened. She told me

she heard a loud bang, as if someone had fallen. AJ came back in
with the first aid kit. Tee told me to sit down and take my shirt off,
so she could bandage the cuts.

I pulled my shirt off and looked at it. I didn't say anything
to them, but looking at the shirt, I knew there was no way those
deep slashes happened by any type of fall from a chair. It looked
as if the two slashes came from some type of claw. I remembered
hearing my name and a snarling sound right before I felt that pain
rip across my back. I looked up at Tee, and she put her arms around
me and told me that I must have fallen and scrapped my back
against the bed railing.

"Guess, I need to be more careful, huh?"

"Yes, you should and you need to get some rest Nova. We
are all worried about Nia too, but we also need to care of our-
selves."

"Yeah, you right girl. AJ, are you okay?"

AJ had a look of disbelief on her face. I don't think she was
buying into the falling off my chair explanation.

"AJ, are you okay?"

"I'm sorry Nova. I don't like the sight of blood. I'm okay."

"It looks much worse than it is. Besides, I have a high toler-
ance for pain. Don't worry about it."

"A'ight Nova. I'm cool."

"So not to change the subject because ya'll know that I like
the attention and all, but I did some research and came up with
several guys that Nia might have been talking to in the last month.
As soon as everybody gets their butts up, we can look at the list."

"Okay Nova, but only if you promise to get some rest girl.
You haven't slept in almost 48 hours. AJ and I will promise to
wake you up when everybody gets up."

"Tee's right. You need to get some zzzz's."

"A'ight girl. Thanks Tee."

I couldn't feel the pain anymore. I guess my body was telling me it needed some rest. I really didn't want to sleep, but I knew I needed it. It wasn't about sleeping, but I wasn't ready for another experience with whatever made those deep scratch marks on me. But, I laid down and before I knew it, I was off dreaming.

There he was standing against my door. He smiled and his dimples appeared. I couldn't take my eyes off his dimples, but I had to look at his light brown eyes. His dimples were so alluring, but his eyes were captivating. When I looked into his eyes, I felt like everything was okay. I felt safe. It was an escape like no other that I have ever felt.

"So, where you been mama? Been waiting for you."
I had so many dreams before of him, but this was the first time I had heard his voice.

"I didn't know you were waiting for me."

"Only fate knows when, but you and I are destined to meet one day."

"Fate? Hmm...How? When? Where?" He said smiling.

"I don't know, but it's all good. Just let things run their course."

"That's easier said than done."

"Trust me."

"Trust someone I don't even know. C'mon now, that smile of yours can only persuade me to a point. I don't know about that trust thing."
He laughed.

"I gotta go mama, but before I forget. You'll find your answers if you start by looking in the most obvious places."

"Wait, don't go. I don't even know your name. Wait!"
I started to reach for him as he turned and walked toward the door.

"Nova, Nova, get up girl!"

AJ was standing next to my bed, as she was shaking me, so I could wake up.

"Dammit girl, ya got the worse timing."

"I'm sorry, but you asked me to wake you up when everybody was up and we're all up, so, my bad."

"It's all good or so he says."

"Huh?"

"Nada girl, nada. Gimme a minute to wash up and I'll be down."

"A'ight, hurry up."

"A'ight."

I washed up in a hurry and rushed downstairs. I remembered I had forgotten the list of screen names, as I got to the bottom of the stairs. I turned around to run back up the stairs, and then AJ yelled at me that she grabbed the list when I went into the bathroom.

"Just like you," I said as I gave her a smirk. AJ knew I was joking with her, so she just laughed at me.

"Alright, that is the list of new friends that Nia added to each of her accounts."

"Where do we go from here Nova?" Rae-Rae said.

"Well, I was thinking since there are about twenty guys on that list, we should each take 3 or 4 screen names and start contacting them through our profile."

"Wait, Nova, I recognize a couple of names on the list."

"Okay Jules, then you take those that you recognize and start there. Keep making contact through your profile, but hit them up with our new profile."

"Same here Nova, I see one I have through YourIt."

"Then do the same Em. Anybody else recognize a name?"

Before we finished dividing up the list there were only about six or seven names that no one knew. I thought this could be a good thing, if Nia's mystery man met her through one of these sites then we might be able to track him down. I kept Maxwell's name to myself. I didn't want any of my girls to know that Nia had him as a friend on her Friendbook. I don't know why, but I thought I should keep it to myself until I found out what was going on. I also told them that I would look into Brackz. I asked AJ to look into DatBoi and PrtiBoi. She agreed. We all looked at each other.

"Well, are we just going to stand around and look at each other all day, or are we going to start searching for our girl?"

Even though we were worried about Nia, we laughed. Luna always has a way of saying things bluntly and abruptly. We all headed in our own direction to get online.

CHAPTER SIX

As I got out of Maxwell's car, I smiled at him and told him good night. He smiled back and waited for me to walk in the building before he drove off. I walked in, turned around, and waved good-bye to him. I watched his car drive off until I couldn't see it anymore. I went up to my room, but before I could get there, Nia opened her door and pulled me into her room.

"So tell me about your date."

"It was cool."

"Get out, Come on, seriously spill it."

"A'ight girl. It was awesome. No, actually, it was almost perfect."

"Details Nova, details."

I laughed because I knew she was dying to know everything that happened. I spent the next several hours talking to Nia about my night. It should have only taken me an hour to tell her everything, but she kept interrupting me and asking questions. She even asked if I slept with Maxwell. I told her that I never kiss and tale. She looked at me and knew I didn't sleep with him. It was actually the only time I can recall that she was listening to me without having an agenda to sneak in her own issues, problems, or situation. We even talked about maybe me moving into her dorm room. I told her that I didn't see a reason to move in because we would soon be living at the sorority house.

By this time, Nia and I both knew that we were all going to

be more than friends. We knew that we were going to be sorority sisters. We just had to get through the time on the line. Soon after, it became a realization. It wasn't easy, but we looked out for each other and went through a lot together, including a hazing incident. We did it though. Luna, Tee, and Rae-Rae were proud of us.

That weekend we went to celebrate at a house party. AJ wasn't even in college yet, but she attended to help her big sis celebrate. She was always where ever Jules was. So, we all hung out together before she actually became a freshman and enrolled at the University. It was a fun night, and we all had a great time. It was the start of something bigger than all of us. It was the start of being our sister's keeper. Nothing would come between any of us.

I decided to forego the remainder of activities that night which was mainly more partying. I headed back to my dorm room. I went in and just laid down. I took out my cell phone. The thought crossed my brain that Maxwell hadn't text me in a couple of days. With classes going on and everything else, I understood that he was probably as busy as I was the past few days. I thought I would call him. The phone rang a couple of times before he answered.

"Hey, I thought you'd never miss me."

"What you talking 'bout?"

"Well, I didn't hit ya up to see how long it would take you to miss me and text or call me."

"Oh, so that's the game you runnin', huh?"

"You funny."

"So, what ya been up to?"

"Not much besides studying, working out, and practicing. Oh, and just one other thing."

"One other thing?"

"Thinking 'bout this shawty I met several weeks back."

"Oh, I see. It's like that. Anybody I know?"

"Could be. I haven't been able to get her out of my head since the night I saw her at the club."

"Hmm...Guess she made quite an impression on you."

"Funny thing, I think I was the one who made quite an impression on her since I moved in on her that night while she was waitin' on a date who never showed up."

"Ha-ha, you funny, and as for you making an impression, well let's just say that the jury is still out on that one."

We both laughed and continued to talk over the next couple of hours. The time went by, and before I knew it, I was waking up the next morning. I fell asleep talking on the phone to Maxwell.

I thought, for sure, as I picked up the phone and placed it to my ear that I would hear a buzzing tone because he had hung up. To my surprise, it was just silent, so I said hello.

"Hey there sleepy head. Did you sleep well? Guess I bored you."

"Oh my gosh, I'm embarrassed Maxwell. My bad."

"Naw, it's cool. The way I see it, I finally got to sleep with you last night."

"Funny!"

"You know what I mean, fall asleep with you. I'm not thinking in a bad way."

"Yeah, I know."

"Well, I gotta get going, but how 'bout we go out tomorrow night?"

"Sure, hit me up later."

"A'ight, I'll get at ya."

I hung up the phone. I got up to start my day. I had a million things to do including finding out what happened at the party after I left. The one person I could count on to fill me in was Nia. I would have to find her after class.

The day went quickly, and I found Nia. She updated me on what I missed at the party. It wasn't much. I told her I would catch up to her later because I had to go to the lab and do some studying. While doing homework, I got bored and logged onto MyProfyle. I had several messages, but I immediately opened the one from Maxwell. He asked if he could pick me up and take me to dinner, then maybe a couple of drinks. Since I had already told him yes, I assumed he was just providing me the details of what he wanted to do. I smiled as the thought of not replying entered my brain. So, that's exactly what I did. I knew he would see that the message was read, but I didn't reply. I was very curious to find out how long it would take for him to contact me about it.

I logged off the site, and the computer. I did enough studying and social networking for the day. I left the lab and started walking back to the dorms. My phone rang. I looked at the caller ID. Not that I was shocked or surprised, but it took him all of ten minutes to contact me. I answered.

"Hey."

"Not cool Nova."

"What?"

"You know."

"I know what?"

"You know and you did it on purpose."

"Maybe."

"No maybes' about it."

"A'ight. It was wrong, but I wanted to hear your voice instead of reading a message."

"I hear ya."

"You better."

"So, tomorrow night, dinner, drinks, and maybe hang out after at my place."

"Uh, what do you mean by hang out after at your place?"

"Just that Ms. Salinas, hang out."

"A'ight. What time should I be ready?"

"Let's say 8 pm."

"Okay, but call me when you're on your way."

"A'ight. I'll hit ya up later."

I've never been much of a talker on the phone, in fact, I liked texting more, but when it came to Maxwell, I liked hearing his voice. It was so sexy. I finally made the long walk back to the dorms. I got to my room and remembered that I made plans to go out with my girls that night. I called Nia to ask what time we were all going out. She told me to be ready by nine because we had to pick up AJ. I told her I would be ready. Since I had a couple of hours to kill, I laid down to get some rest.

I must have fallen asleep because I awoke to my phone ringing. It was Nia, and she was asking if I was almost ready. I looked at the time, and I had forty-five minutes to get dressed. I threw on a pair of jeans, a Guess top, my favorite Guess shoes, and polished the look off with a few accessories. I checked myself in the mirror, and then walked over to Nia's room. Em and Jules were already there.

"Hey girl, it's 'bout time."

"Yeah, my bad Em, but I fell asleep."

"It's all good girl 'cause Nia just finished gettin' ready."

"Hey Jules. Is your sis ready?"

"Yeah, girl has been blowing up my phone."

"A'ight, let's roll then. C'mon Nia, you texted me forty-five

minutes ago rushin' me and ya wasn't even ready yourself."

"Yeah, Yeah, I'm ready. How do I look?"

"Whatever, you know you look great. You just wanna hear it. Let's go."

We headed out to Nia's SUV and made our way over to Jules's dad's house to pick up AJ. She waited outside and hurried to the SUV as we drove up.

"My girls. What's up?"

"Shut up AJ. Did you tell dad that you were gonna hang with me tonight?"

"Naw, just told him I was going out."

"Good. I don't want him blowing up my phone at 2 am asking where you at."

"Whatev'r Jules."

Em laughed. Jules was always giving AJ a hard time, but she'd have her back in a second if anybody gave her little sis any crap. Nia had already decided to check out the Ultra Lounge downtown that we had hung out at before. We liked the place because it had a cool atmosphere. We got there and had to wait a couple of minutes to get in. We'd probably have waited longer if Jules didn't work her magic and flirt with the bouncer at the door.

We made our way over to one of the VIP sections. We decided to chill there. The place didn't have a dance floor, but we didn't need one because we would just dance in the area we were at. We were having a good time. We were laughing, dancing, and just checking out the scenery. A group of guys made their way over to us and starting talking. They were pretty cool and asked if they could get us a round of shots. Of course, we told them yes. The shots were brought over to us, and as I was about to down it, I noticed out of the corner of my eyes that Maxwell was standing on

the far side, at the rear, of the bar. He smiled and nodded his head.
I smiled back and downed my shot.

"Hey, Imma take a walk. I'll be back."

"Hey girl, where are you going?"

"I'll be right back, Nia."

"Alright, don't do anything I wouldn't do."

"You crazy girl."

I walked back around to the side and made my way back up to the front, then toward the back to get to the restrooms. I could have just walked straight to the back, but then I'd have to pass by Maxwell and his boys. I just wasn't going to do that. I didn't want to crowd him and besides I had plans to see him tomorrow night. By the time, I made my way to the restrooms, Maxwell was already standing there.

"So, what's up? You avoiding me?"

"Naw, just trying to get to the restroom."

"Woulda been easier if you didn't take the long way 'round."

"Yeah, I know."

"So, what's up?"

"Nada, just here with my girls."

"Cool. I'm doing the same. Just chillin' with the homies."

"I see."

"So, how 'bout I buy you a drink and we chill for a lil' while."

"I don't know. I don't wanna mess up your plans for the night."

"I see. Well you ain't, but if you don't wanna hang then cool."

"It's not like that. I'm mean we got plans tomorrow night,

so you can do your thing tonight."

"You're funny Nova. Let's take a walk."

"A'ight."

We left through the restroom entrance, walked through the hallway, and around the corner to enter the connecting lounge on the other side of the building. I didn't even know that hallway lead to another Ultra Lounge. We walked through the lounge and made our way out the front door of the place.

"So, where to?"

"Does it really matter Nova? Cause for me, it's not about the destination, but rather the person I'm taking with me."

Maxwell had a way of making me blush. And that was unlike me. His words seemed to be real. I didn't feel like he was lying or playin' me. We strolled down Commerce Street as we talked. We were talking about everything and nothing. We walked over to the most famous tourist attraction in San Antonio, the River walk. The River walk is exactly what it sounds like. It's a pathway along the river in the middle of downtown. It stretches for miles and several hotels, restaurants, and shops are located on its path. At night, the River walk lights up, and it's quite a beautiful scenery. I've walked the River walk at least a hundred times before, but tonight walking along its path was breath taking, and I can only assume that had to do with the company I was keeping.

We walked for a couple of hours and continued to talk about things. I didn't want the night to end, but it was almost last call. We decided to get back to the Ultra Lounge. We arrived and I looked at Maxwell. He knew I didn't want the night to end. However, I couldn't risk continuing the night with him. I really liked Maxwell, and I knew it was too early and risky to get caught up in a physical relationship with him.

"Can I kiss you Nova?"

"I don't know if that's really a good idea right now, but honestly I don't think I can say no to you."

He leaned in and gave me the most soft and sensual kiss that I ever felt. It was like lightning striking me for a second time. I felt a sensation rip through every inch of my body. At that moment, I knew that I was under his spell.

"Let me walk you back inside, and then I'll say good-night."

"Oh, so you playin' hard to get now, huh?" I laughed as I winked at him.

"No need for playin' games with a girl like you, but I ain't easy either."
He winked back at me and smiled.

"Good cause neither am I."

"Nice Ms. Salinas, and I will leave it at this...there's no point in a chase when someone makes it too easy."

"You crazy."

Maxwell walked me back inside and over to where my girls were still standing and dancing.

"Hey ya'll. This is Maxwell."

"What's up Maxwell?"

"Hi Maxwell, nice to meet you."

"Hey, how's it going?"

"Yeah, what's up?"

"Hey, what's up ladies?"

Maxwell met everyone and then told me he had to get back to his boys because he rode over with them. He hugged me and whispered in my ear that he had a great time and was looking forward to our date tomorrow. He walked away.

It was last call and my girls had enough to drink. I made the call that I would be the designated driver since I had one drink all night. AJ's phone was blowing up. Her dad was texting and calling her every five minutes and she just kept ignoring it. We left, so we could take her home. We dropped her off and headed back to the dorm. Next thing, it was morning.

I opened my eyes and looked around the room. I couldn't remember any dreams I may have had during the night. It was unusual for me not to remember at least one dream. I picked up my phone and saw that I missed a text from Maxwell. He text me as he did every morning to tell me to have a great day. I was wondering if Maxwell had any bad qualities because he seemed too good to be true. I stayed in bed for another hour just reminiscing about the night I had with him. I started to wonder what our date night was going to be like. Maxwell had been a perfect gentleman so far, and I wonder if that would change in anyway tonight. He seemed unlike other guys I dated in the past, who pressured me for sex after a while of dating or hanging out. There was really no point in driving myself crazy about the issue. It wasn't like I could tell the future, even though I did see things in my dreams. I would just have to let things play out with Maxwell and see what happened.

I decided to get up and go to the gym to work out. It was a quick fix for stress of any kind. I would probably run into Jules. She was always working out. I think she lived in the gym. I text Nia and asked if she wanted to go. She agreed, and I knew I would be drilled about last night. I got dressed and walked over to her room. I knocked and she came out in the cutest pink warm-up suit.

"You goin' to work out or what?"

"Shut up...what's wrong with this?"

"Ugh, nothing if you tryin' to impress some hottie."

"Girl, you never know who's going to be at the gym."

"True."

We walked over to the university gym. I was actually shocked that Nia hadn't asked about anything yet. As I got on the elliptical, she started her inquiry.

"So, what happened to you last night?"

"What are you talking 'bout?"

"Please, you told me you were gonna be right back, and then you were gone all night."

"Nothing happened. I went to the restroom and I ran into Maxwell and we hung out."

"Oh, okay. You're boy comes along and you ditch us."

"C'mon girl. It was not like that. I didn't ditch anybody. Honestly, ya'll was having fun with those guys. I didn't think it would be a big deal."

"I guess."

"Ya know I'm right. You just having an issue because it was Maxwell. Had it been another guy, you wouldn't be acting like this."

"Whatever."

"Girl, you need to stop. He's cool. I like him."

"Really?"

"Yeah, I do."

"Alright, I'll be cool about it, but doesn't mean I have to like him."

"Yeah, I know that too." Nia and I worked out for the next hour. She didn't talk about Maxwell again, but she did tell me about her and Marcos getting to really know each other. They had been going out for a while since they met. It seemed like she really liked him.

Nia decided she was done exercising. I still had some stress I needed to work out, so I told her I was going to stay around the gym for a little while longer. She looked at me like I was crazy. She told me she was going to hit the shower, then get back to the dorm to get dressed, and take off for her visit home with her mom. She had planned to stay there the weekend. I told her I would her give a call tomorrow since I had plans with Maxwell tonight.

I went over to abs machine and started to work out on that. I looked up and across the gym I thought I saw Maxwell working out. My eyes were straining to see if it was him. I couldn't really tell, but, if it wasn't, the person had features that resembled his remarkably. I kept working out and looking in his direction. He started to walk over my way. As he got closer, I noticed it wasn't Maxwell. I felt silly. I wonder if my mind was playing tricks on me again or if I actually had him on my brain that intensely. Either way, I was done exercising for the day. I walked toward the showers and ran into Jules as she was getting ready for her daily routine.

"Hey girl, good to see you here. Oh yeah, Maxwell's cute."

"Hey Jules, what's up? Yeah, I kinda think so too."

"Any plans to see him soon?"

"Actually, I need to get a shower and get ready for my date with him tonight."

"You go girl. Hey, for what it's worth...he seemed like he really liked you. I mean regardless what anybody else says."

"Oh, I hear ya. Thanks."

"Alright, I got to hit the gym. See ya later girl."

"Yeah, talk to ya later."

I couldn't stop thinking about the comment that Jules made about "regardless what anybody else says". I knew who she was

talking about without her having to say it. I wondered exactly what
Nia had been telling them. I knew what she was saying wasn't bad
since she was my girl. I figured she was just trying to look out for
me.

I got back to the dorms and started trying to figure out what
I was going to wear. I pulled out some destroyed jeans and Marci-
ano top. I looked over my shoe selection, and, of course, pulled out
a pair of Guess shoes. All I had to do was flat iron my hair, do my
make-up, and accessorize the outfit. I was ready to go. My phone
rang.

"Hello."

"Why so formal?"

"I don't know."

"Well, are you ready? I've got an interesting night
planned."

"Interesting?"

"Yeah, but no details just yet."

"Okay. Yes, I'm ready and I do look good tonight."

"Uh-Uh...you look good all the time."

"Whatev'r...I'm ready."

"A'ight. Be there in ten minutes."

"A'ight."

I was waiting by the window and looking out for Maxwell
to drive up. I saw the headlights pull up to the front of the building.
I walked downstairs, by the time I got to the door he was standing
there.

"Wow, I didn't hear you knock."

"That's 'cause I was just about too."

"Oh, I see."

"I should say wow. You look amazing."

"Thanks."

"Let's go."

"Where are we going?"

*"What did I tell you about the destination of places...
doesn't matter as long as I'm taking you with me."*

*"I remember. A'ight. Let's go then." We walked out to
his car. He opened the door for me. It felt strange that he always
opened doors for me, especially since he was only nineteen. I didn't
know many guys his age that would open doors for their dates.
Then again, I didn't know any guys any age that did that. Maxwell was younger than me, but he seemed so much more mature
for his age. I couldn't put my finger on it, but there was something
definitely different about him. He seemed perfect, and had my full
attention at this point. The only other man that I knew who came
close to capturing my attention was the one from my dream. The
only problem with that was I didn't know who he was.*

*We arrived at a private airport. I looked at Maxwell and
didn't know what to think.*

"Should I be worried?"

"Worried. What do you mean?"

*"We're at an airport. You do know that I told my girls that I
had a date with you?"*

*"Funny Nova. I'm only gonna kidnap you for an hour or
two, and then I'll have you back in S.A. so we can hang out at my
place for the rest of the night. I promise."*

"Oh ok, but just a warning...I have my mace on me."

*Maxwell laughed as he led me onto his private plane owned
by his parents. In fact, he told me later that night that his family owned the private airport. I knew that Maxwell's family had
money, but I didn't realize how much money they actually had until*

*tonight. We flew to Houston, Texas, which was about a forty-five
minute flight. A driver was waiting for us as we arrived.*

"Wow, Houston...big time."

"Sorry, I know it's not New York, or Vegas, or even Holly-
wood, but I wanted Jamaican cuisine and there's a restaurant that
I really like to eat at. Do you mind?"

"Of course not, I'm joking with ya...honestly, H-Town is my
dad's hometown. It's a cool place."

"Cool. Let's get going."

*We got into a hummer. Even though Maxwell had money,
he didn't like to act as if he did. Yes, he had the nice cars, home,
and everything else, but he didn't act like he was all that. He lived
like the rest of us lived. We drove to the south side of town and
pulled into a strip. We pulled up to a small place. It was a hole in
the wall. I started to realize that Maxwell was full of surprises.
We went in and sat at the bar. The waitress and cook knew him by
name. He introduced me to them. They were nice people. I assumed
they were married to each other.*

"You can have anything you like."

"I've never had Jamaican cuisine before."

"Oh, I see. Interesting."

"What is?"

"This is a first for you."

"I guess, so then I'll leave it up to you as to what to order."

"Are you sure? Cause you have one of everything and decide what you like."

"No...that's alright, just order for me please."

"A'ight." *Maxwell began to order. We both had a beer
while we waited for our food.*

"Tell me about your dad."

"Not a whole lot to tell. I didn't really know him. He was gone a lot when I was growing up."

"We live in S.A. and he was always in Houston working or so my mom said."

"Oh okay, well if you don't want to talk about it. It's cool."

"Naw, I'm okay talking about it. Supposedly I have family here, but I don't really know them."

"Oh, I see."

"What about your mom? Any siblings?"

"You ask a lot of questions."

"Isn't that what you do when you like someone and want to get to know them better."

"Oh, so you like me?" Just then our food was brought over to us.

"I hope you enjoy Nova. This is one of my favorite places in town."

"Only one way to find out." We began to eat. The food was extraordinary. I savored every bite. It was a perfect meal. It was my first taste of Jamaican food. It might have been a hole in the wall, but the fullness of flavor in which the meal consisted made it a five star restaurant in my book. Maxwell was pleased that I enjoyed his pick of restaurant and food choice. He thanked the couple for their hospitality and tipped them hugely. They told me it was their pleasure to meet me and invited me back anytime I was in town. I told them I hoped to be back soon.

"I can make that happen. All you gotta do is ask."

"I'm sure you can Maxwell. Thank you for a wonderful meal. I really enjoyed myself."

"You're not calling it a night already are you?"

"No, I'm not."

"Good, cause it just started."

"So, where too...oops. I know, doesn't really matter."

"You learn quick."

"Yeah, I do."

Maxwell and I got into the vehicle. He didn't say where we were going. He just drove. In fact, we drove around the city. He was pointing out different places and telling me about them. He said we would come back and hit a couple of the spots on our next visit. I was a little shocked to hear him talk about the future and me in it. If he noticed, he didn't say anything. He kept driving. The city was beautiful at night, but I always had this vision of everything being more beautiful at night. I don't know why, but it just was.

We headed back to the small airport we arrived at in Houston. We boarded back onto his family's plane, and headed back to San Antonio. We arrived forty-five minutes later. His BMW was ready for us when we landed. We got into his car, and he drove us back to his place. He invited me inside. He asked me if I wanted anything to drink. I wasn't sure that was a good idea, but I accepted his offer and asked for a glass of Mascato. He poured me a glass and led me into the media room. I had seen the room the first time I was visiting, but it was different sitting in there. It was like he had his own theater in his home.

"The movie should start in a couple of minutes."

"Now are you tryin' to impress me."

"Is it working?"

"Nope...all my dates do this for me."

"Oh, I see. Hmm...I'll think bigger next time."

"Whateva Maxwell. On the real, I had a great time tonight. Thank you."

"You're welcome Nova."

We sat back. The lights began to dim. The movie started. Maxwell put his arm around me and pulled me up next to him. It was comfortable that close to him. We didn't exchange words as we watched the movie. As the movie ended, it was nearly three in the morning.

"You should stay here tonight."

"That's not a good idea."

"I just want you to stay and sleep. Nothing more."

"I don't know."

"I wouldn't put anything on you that you wouldn't want to do."

"I know you wouldn't. Okay."

Maxwell led me up to the west wing and into the master bedroom, which was his room. His room was probably as big as the house I grew up in. He had a king size bed that looked like it was made for a king.

"Do you have a t-shirt or something I can sleep in?"

"Of course, let me get it for you."

Maxwell walked over to his huge walk-in closet and pulled a t-shirt off a hanger. I took the shirt and walked into the bathroom to change. I came out and he was lying in the bed. I walked over and got into his bed.

"Don't worry Nova. This is your game. I'm just an opponent who's playin' by the rules. It may be my court, but the ball's in your hand."

I didn't feel nervous laying next Maxwell. I moved over closer to him as he wrapped his arm around me. I laid my head down upon his chest. The rhythm of his heartbeat eased me to sleep.

CHAPTER SEVEN

I went back up to my room to log on to MyProfyle.com. I went into my messages and searched for the message from Brackz. It took me a couple of minutes to find it. I opened the message and hit the reply button. I introduced myself to him. I gave him several details about who I was and what I was about. I told him that I was a huge music fan and that I love listening to music, so I found him very interesting. I tried to keep the message short and to the point. I didn't want to over kill it by writing to much about me. I pushed the send button and off it went. It would be a waiting game now.

I clicked back over to my friend's list and checked who was online. I figured I might as well do some social networking while I was online. I noticed that Maxwell was on. I wanted to send him an instant message, IM, but after the falling out we had I knew I needed some time and space. We had a huge argument a couple of nights before Nia went missing. In fact, it was Nia who really had more of a blow up with him than I did. I was going to ignore the whole issue, but she kept telling me that I couldn't let him off the hook. That night was crazy, and I knew she was just getting my back, being her sister's keeper, but I wished she would have kept out of it.

I saw all the girls online, so I knew they were busy making contact with the guys on their part of the list. I could only hope that whatever we were doing would work and lead us in the right direction to find Nia. It was still so unbelievable that she was missing.

What was even more unbelievable was that she didn't tell anyone about the guy she was talking to. Nia couldn't keep a secret even if her life depended on it.

We all knew this, it just wasn't in her character to keep secrets especially if it was about her. I know she wanted to tell me about the guy she met online, but my head kept wondering why she waited so long to try to tell me about it. I knew I was missing something, but I just couldn't figure it out. Every time Nia met someone, she immediately told me about him or told one of the girls. She always wanted my opinion about it even though I always told her I was no expert in relationships. It didn't matter to her because she valued my opinion for some reason.

As I sat there in thought and looking at the computer screen, AJ sent me an IM letting me know that she made contact with DatBoi and sent a message to PrtiBoi. I responded asking her to keep me in the loop. I told her that Nia had both of these users on MyProfyle and YourIt. I was curious to find out who these two guys were because neither of them had a profile picture up on either site. AJ responded that she would let me know later because she was in a conversation at the moment with DatBoi. I replied for her to find out anything she could about him especially his real name. She didn't reply back which meant that she was trying to do exactly that.

A message notification popped up on my screen. I had received a message from a friend. I clicked over to my message folder. It was from Brackz. I didn't expect for him to get back to me as soon as he did since it took me a couple of weeks to reply to his message. I opened it and read the message. He replied telling me that he was finally glad to hear from me. He wasn't sure if I going to ever respond, and was surprised when he received my message today. I didn't know how to explain my reasoning for waiting several weeks before getting back to him. I thought I would just tell him a little white lie, even though I hated liars, it was for good cause. I replied and told him that I was in a relationship and I recently split up, so I wasn't ready to talk or get into something else with anybody. I sent the message to him. I had no idea that my little white lie was going to be the full blown truth.

AJ ran into the room. She had a look on her face like she was about to drop the worst news possible on her best friend. But since her best friend wasn't in the room with us, I had no idea what was going on.

"Don't freak out."

"What ya talkin' 'bout?"

"DatBoi…Nova, I don't know how to say this."

"Say what? AJ just say whatever you need to."

"Maxwell."

"What 'bout Maxwell?"

"DatBoi…it's Maxwell."

"What?"

"I was talking to him on the IM. We were having a conversation and I was trying to do exactly what you asked. So, I starting asking questions about him. How old he was, where he lived, what school he went to. When he told me all that, he asked if maybe would could chill sometime. I told him I didn't know who he was or even what he looked like because he didn't have a picture on his profile. He told me he would send me one if I would send him one too. So, I told him sure, but to send me one first. He did. It was Maxwell."

"What the f is going on AJ? I didn't tell you or the girls, but Nia has Maxwell on her friend's list on Friendbook." At that moment, I knew something more was going on between Maxwell and Nia, but I had no clue what it was.

"I don't understand Nova. Nia can't stand Maxwell. Honestly neither can I, but I didn't want you to know that."

"Yeah, I know you don't like him. I know even more that Nia hated him. So, your guess girl is as good as mine. But, Imma 'bout to get to the bottom of this."

"What are you gonna do?"

"I don't know just yet. Do me a favor, don't tell anybody 'bout this, A'ight?"

"A'ight. Do you want me to keep contacting him."

"Naw, let me figure things out." AJ left my room to leave me with my thoughts. I noticed a message notification. It was from Brackz. He asked if had an IM because it would be easier to talk. I replied right back and gave him my user name for my IM so he could add me. Within a couple of minutes I accepted him as a friend. The IM screen popped up and we were chatting.

His was asking questions about me. It was the same conversation all opposite sexes have when they meet. It was the "let's get to know each other" talk. Brackz and I spent a couple of hours on the IM. He was actually a very interesting character. Although, I knew there was an underlining reason for getting to know him, I actually thought he was very cool. There was a six-hour difference in our time zones, so he asked me if he could talk to me again later because he needed to get some sleep. I accepted his offer to continue our conversation at another time, and said good night.

As I was going to log off for the evening, I received another message notification. I clicked open the inbox and it was from Maxwell. I opened it. He asked if he could text or call me because he wanted to talk. I was actually shocked since the last time I saw him in the club, it was a bad falling out between us, and Nia made it worse. I sent a message back to him saying it was fine to contact me. At that moment, I realized that Maxwell always had a strange way of contacting me when I was talking to another guy or if I met someone new. It was like he had some kind of radar or instinct which told him that someone was trying to get to know me. It was crazy. My phone rang.

"Hello."

"Why so formal?"

"I'm not sure. What's up?"

"I thought maybe we should talk about it."

"There's nothing really to talk about."

"Are you okay?"

"Yeah, it's not like I have a claim on you."

"I know. Just making sure you okay."

"Yeah. I shouldn't have went off on you. And Nia had no right to make that scene up in the club."

"Yeah, you're right. You didn't and she sure in the hell didn't have no right at all."

"Yeah, I said I know. So, what do you want?"

"Honestly, I think we should end this."

"End what? We've been talking off and on."

"Yeah, I thought maybe we could chill again like we use to, but I don't think it will work out."

"It's cool Maxwell. Don't worry we can just be friends."

"No, you don't understand Nova. We can't be friends either."

"What do you mean?"

"I'm sorry Nova."

"Are you serious? It was your idea to remain friends. This

whole thing from the day you first contacted me on MyProfyle was your idea. Meeting me was your idea. Hanging out with me was your idea. Dating me was your idea. It was your idea and now after all this time, me remaining your friend after everything you did to me, now you decide that we need to end whatever this is?"

"Look, we just need to end this. You don't want any part of me because it wouldn't be good for you. You would get hurt when it's all done."

"Whatever Maxwell. I'll see ya 'round." I hung up the phone before he said anything else. I was furious at him. I didn't know what to think about what he told me. It was strange and out of nowhere. Maxwell and I remained friends even after I saw him with other girls. We stopped hanging out with each other after that summer Freshman year, that Nia and I went down to Corpus, but we still talked throughout our sophomore year. I never went back to his house again, and we never had sex after that one and only time. Things were never really the same after that, and I had no explanation as to why.

I laid down on my bed. I kept thinking about things with Maxwell. What happened? I never really understood why he distant himself from me after that night we made love. I thought it was something I did. Maybe it was because I couldn't remember the entire night, even though I tried to remember it. The funny thing was that I only had three drinks that night. I've never passed out on three drinks before. I couldn't make any sense of it. I played all the events up until that night in my head. I knew Maxwell liked me as much as I liked him. He even gave me that gift afterwards which I still had. It was my favorite piece of jewelry. I must have thought about everything over and over before my eyes grew tired…

"Hey lil' girl. It's been quite a while. Look at you! You're all grown up."

"Oh my gosh!"

"Is that all you got for your ol' man?"

"Dad." I called out as my eyes tear up, and realized I couldn't get any other words out as I was so surprised to see him again.

"You stop that now...I won't have my lil' girl crying over any man, and that includes her father."

"Where you been? I haven't seen or heard from you in years? I should be so mad at you for going away like that."

"I haven't gone anywhere. You know I've been right here as I always am when you need me, so here I am."

"I'm not sure what you mean Dad."

"Lil' girl, I'll always be close by to protect you. You are the last of my blood, and I can't have anything happen to you."

"The last of your blood?"

"You have to remember. It's the only thing that will protect you from those who mean to harm you."

"Dad, you're not making any sense...the last?...harm? What are you talking about?"

"When you remember, it will all make sense. I've got to go now. You have to remember who you are. Go back, back to your childhood, back to the place when dreams made sense. When you get there, everything will no longer be dark."

"Dad, don't go!"

"Hush now...you'll be okay. You're strong Nova, and no one or nothing can ever harm you. All you have to do is realize who you truly are. Take care lil' girl." As he said those words, I woke up from out of the dream in a cold sweat.

I got up from the computer desk, and went over to my bed to lay down. I laid there with my mind racing a hundred miles an hour. My mind was jumping from thinking about the dream of my Dad and what it all meant, to Maxwell and the break-up, to Nia and wondering if she was ok or would we find out the worst, to Brackz. I laid there and couldn't fall asleep. My mind kept going back to those words, "remember who you are". I didn't talk much about my dreams to anyone, but I knew I had to talk to my mom. I remembered a lot about my childhood, but there were so many empty spaces I couldn't fill with memories. I remember asking my mom on several occasions about my childhood and lost memories of certain ages in my life, but all she ever really told me was that I was a happy child and enjoyed every moment in growing up.

My email notification alarm sounded off, and I got up, looked over at the time, and realized it was 3am, and I stilled couldn't sleep. I walked over to the computer, and opened my email. It was Brackz. I smiled, and started to read his email. It was a flattering email, and he went on about how he couldn't get me off his mind, and how we seem to hit it off as if we were meant to meet. He said he felt like we were soul mates or knew each other from a prior life. I didn't believe much in past lives, but his word flowed so smoothly across the page that I found myself reading it twice, and wondering if there was an afterlife. If there was, I definitely was interested in hearing more about it from him.

I emailed him back, and started a conversation. In doing so, we emailed back and forth the entire morning, and before I knew it, I forgot about the underlining reason of why I was talking him. I was laughing by myself, and having a great conversation with someone from across the world. I wasn't sure if it was the conversation or if I just talked myself into thinking Brackz couldn't be involved with the disappearance of Nia. I mean, after all, he was half way around the world, so how could he have played any part in it?

I ended our conversation around 6am. I told him I had to get some sleep, and probably would be skipping classes that day. He asked if he could have my number, and if I said yes, he would call me at a reasonable time, which meant he would have to stay up late to call. I didn't see any harm in that, but I wasn't sure if I wanted to pursue this any further than it had already gone. I still had Maxwell on my mind, and I didn't want to jump into any-thing else even though he didn't deserve me to give him a second thought. I was ready to get out there again, and starting dating, and meeting new people, but I thought what good would it do me to try and date someone in another continent.

I asked Brackz if we could keep our conversations limited to email and IM for the time being. As I sent off my last email for the morning, I hoped he understood my reasoning, and I waited for a response. He responded immediately, and said he had no problem in keeping our new friendship via the net until I felt more comfort-able with him. I didn't respond anymore after that, but I did notice an email from an unknown source. I opened it up and it was from someone I didn't know, but he claimed to know me. It was an invite to a social network site. I never heard of the site itself, but it had an interesting name. It was called Hookup.com. For a minute, I was intrigued, but too tired to look into it.

I laid down on my bed, and soon I was drifting back off to that place so familiar…dreamland. *And there he was…*

"*Hey ma.*"

"*Hey stranger. It so good to see you again.*"

"*I thought you might never let me back in. It's been so long since we last spoke."*

> *"Yessir, it has been."*

> *"Regardless, it's good to see you, and that smile of yours."*

> *"C'mon now, you gonna make me blush here."*

> *"You're funny mama. You know why I'm here though, don't*
you?"

> *"I'm not sure, but I have feeling you're the reason I need to*
know who I truly am."

> *"Our time is around the corner...you just have to look in*
the right place."

> *"Why is everyone talking in riddles?"*
He smiled.

> *"You'll know when the time comes."*
I smiled back and winked at him.

> *"If you say so."*

> *"Time here is almost up ma, but our time has yet begun.*
You need to go to sleep now...soon enough, I'll see you."

> *"Wait..."*

I woke to my phone ringing. I didn't answer it. All I could think about in that minute, was this man in my dreams. I never got his name, but his smile and dimples were so vividly clear. I had slept through the morning and into the afternoon. I went out into the hall, and into the bathroom to wash up. I went downstairs into the common area. No one was around. I figured everyone was in class. I went into the kitchen, and grabbed a bite to eat. I went back upstairs, and got dressed. I was free that day since I didn't attend classes, but I knew I could get notes from friends.

I decided to get back online, but not to do any social networking or so I thought. I was curious about that site. I was also curious about the person who also sent it. I looked up Hookup.

com. The site was for singles looking to do just that, hook up with no strings attached. I probably wouldn't have given the site any real attention, but I was on mission to get over Maxwell. The only way I knew how to do that was to meet people and have plenty of superficial relationships. I was pretty good at superficial relationships, and I had every intention of becoming an expert at it, so I created a profile.

I planned to look through some of the profiles of guys on the site, but before I could, I received and instant message from Brackz. I instantly smiled, and logged off the site and jumped on the mesenger to talk to him. As always, he was such a charmer. The crazy thing was that I usually didn't pay much attention to smooth talkers, but he was somewhat different. He was charming, but he had a sincere tone in the words he wrote. I asked him how the music thing was going for him. He said he just got back from recording in the studio, and went on to ask if I would like to hear a sample of his music. I messaged him back with one word…sure.

He sent me a file via the messenger, and I downloaded and played it. It was interesting, cool, and I liked it. I told him exactly that. We chatted for several hours about things of interest, past relationships, and what each of us was looking for in the opposite sex. It was a good conversation, and the time flew by, but I couldn't stay up all night again with him. I said my good nights, and I logged off the messenger.

At that moment, Maxwell came across my mind, and before I could stop myself, I picked up my phone and sent him a text message. An hour had gone by, and I was finding myself getting upset that he did not reply, so I jumped back on to Hookup.com. As soon as I logged on, I noticed several messages from different guys. I started to read some of the messages, and started to reply back. The messages kept coming from different guys. In the moment, I had forgotten all about Maxwell, and started replying back. Most of the messages were quick and short. After all it was a site for people who wanted no strings attached, and the guys were not shy about wanting only one thing. I was just having some fun in meeting and talking to different guys, and before I knew it I had several first dates scheduled. Not only did I forget about Maxwell, but I forgot about Nia as well.

CHAPTER EIGHT

I woke up that morning to find myself alone in bed. I sat up and looked around his room, but he was nowhere in sight. I got up, went to the restroom, and got dressed. There was a note on the mirror letting me know that he had to go out and didn't want to wake me. He left me a toothbrush and toothpaste on the sink, so I could wash up. I made my way downstairs. An older gentleman approached me. I didn't know who he was.

"I'm Mr. Brenan's assistant. He apologizes for not being able to take you home, but he wants me to make sure that you get home safely. Would you like breakfast Nova?"

"Uh...no thanks. I would just like to get home."

"Okay ma'am. Let me pull the car around."

I was a little disappointed in Maxwell for leaving me alone in his home. Although I didn't know the reason behind it, I felt unimportant. I went outside to the front, and the car came around and I got in the back seat. Thoughts were racing through my head, as I felt a little embarrassed about being driven home by a total stranger.

Before we arrived at the dorms, my cell phone rang. I answered it.

"Hello."

"Why so formal?"

"I don't know. You tell me Maxwell."

"I'm sorry I wasn't there when you got up this morning.

You looked so peaceful and I didn't want to wake you up. I'm actually on campus right now."

"It's all good."

"Let me make it up to you. I'll be done in an hour or two. Let's have lunch and spend the day together."

"I don't know. I have some things I have to do."

"Like what?"

"Homework, studying, you know the college thing."

"Then meet me at the lab. I'll help you and after we can grab a bite to eat and hang out. Please."

"I must be outta my mind, but okay. I'll see you at the lab in an hour. Bye."

I hung up the phone and didn't wait for him to say bye to me. The driver pulled up to the front of the dorms and I got out. I thanked him for getting me home as I closed the door. I walked up to my dorm. I was going to stop at Nia's room and talk to her, but I remember she was staying the weekend at her mom's house. I went to get a change of clothing and take a shower. I got dressed and went over to the lab.

As I walked in, Maxwell was sitting there and smiled at me. He got up and went to meet me at the front by the entrance.

"Hey, I'm really sorry about this morning. I promise that will never happen again."

"Yeah, you right about that."

"What's that suppose to mean."

"Next time I won't be so quick to stick around."

"Don't do that. I did have a good reason for leaving..."

"It's all good I said...no big deal."

"Wow, I didn't realize you were going to be this upset about it."

"I'm not. Let's forget about it. I need to study."

We walked over to the computers and we sat down. Maxwell looked at me, then pulled me toward him to hug me. As soon as his arm went around me, I forgot about the whole morning thing. I didn't tell him that though. He helped me study for a couple of hours. I actually got a lot of homework done. He was very smart and I was considering making him my tutor.

"Let's get outta here."

"A'ight."

"You didn't ask where we are going."

"It's not about the destination Maxwell. It's about being my choice in wanting to go and with whom I want to go with."

"I like that Ms. Salinas."

We left the lab and walked to his car. He drove us to some small Italian restaurant. We sat there for a couple hours and talked. I never questioned him about that morning. I figured if he was on campus, his leaving me alone must have been important and had something to do with school. We spent the entire day together just hanging out. He dropped me off early that night since we had classes in the morning.

That night, I had dreams as I did almost every night. Except these dreams were a little darker. I couldn't make any sense of them. And then he showed up. It was my dream guy. I didn't know what else to call him not knowing his name.

"Hey you."

"Hey ma. Did you forget about me?"

"Of course not, but I've been a little busy lately."

"Yeah, I know. He's been pulling you away from me."

"Who?"

"Your latest admirer. I haven't seen you because of him. He

doesn't want anyone around you."

"So, how does that include you since you're just a figment of my imagination."

"Am I?"

"Yes, I think so. I've never met you and yet you visit me on a regular basis.

Wouldn't you consider that a figment of my imagination."

"I consider it something bigger than the both of us."

"I'm not sure what you mean."

"Just don't forget about me. Be careful of those that you're surrounded by. Things aren't always what they seem."

"I know you're about to disappear again, but I have a request."

"What is it mama?"

"Find me."

With that last thing said, I woke up in a cold sweat. I was starting to remember more of my dreams. They were getting intense and darker. Before it was just bits and pieces, here and there, but now I was remembering several dreams a night. I even recalled a dream about my childhood. I hadn't dreamed about my childhood in so long.

I was lying there thinking about what the dream guy had told me about my latest admirer. Was he talking about Maxwell? I wasn't sure, but I couldn't let a guy in my dream get in the way of something great that I had going with Maxwell. That would be ridiculous. What would I tell Maxwell? I can't date you anymore because there's this guy in my dream who is warning me that you're not good for me. Oh yeah, and by the way, I don't even know who he is, but he's the reason I can't continue this with you. Maxwell would think I was crazy, and I was starting to think I was too. So, I put it out of my mind, and got up to start a new week.

Maxwell and I continued to see each other after that. We texted daily and talked on the phone several times a week. We went out on dates at least once a week. School, friends, and other things kept us busy, but we always made time to hang out with each other. Six months went by and, in that time, I didn't see my dream guy again. I kept dreaming, but he never came to me again. I thought to myself that I created my dream guy to be my safety net. A safety net that would catch me if Maxwell and I didn't work out. It made sense.

Maxwell and I kept our relationship platonic the entire time we were dating. During those six months, I went over to his house several times, but I never stayed again. I didn't want to ever wake up again feeling like I did that one morning I woke up alone in his home. With every day that passed, we grew closer and closer. I knew the time would eventually come to take our relationship to next level. In fact, I was ready for it to go there and so was Maxwell. We had already discussed it, but he told me he could wait until I was sure I was ready to go there with him. At this point, I was sure I was ready. I had even talked about it with Nia and AJ.

Both Nia and AJ advised me to give it some more time. I looked at them like they were crazy. I had already given it well over six months. Our Freshman year was almost over.

"Look, I really like him. You both know that. I've told you everything that has gone on between him and I since day one."

"Yeah, but you know that once you have sex with him things will change."

"Really Nia, really? You're gonna stand there and give me advice on guys."

"We're just looking out for you Nova. I just don't have a

good feeling about him."

"I don't see why AJ. Besides, who's gonna sleep with him you or me?"

"Ugh! Dammit Nova, I know you're going to do what you want. So, just use protection."

"You funny girl. That's why we tight. Don't worry 'bout me. I know what I want."

"Use protection...really Nia? Like she doesn't know that. Who are you, her mom?"

"No, her sister's keeper, but you don't know nothing about that...do you AJ?"

We laughed. I knew their intentions were good, but they didn't know Maxwell like I did. Jules came up to our room and told AJ that she had to take her back home already. We forgot that AJ was still in high school. She was going to be a senior when the fall semester started, but she couldn't wait to get to college. That was mainly our fault. She hung out with us too much.

AJ walked out the room as she told us bye. Nia went downstairs to grab something to snack on. I picked up my phone and texedt Maxwell. I sent him a text asking him what he was doing. He replied to me that he was thinking about me. I smiled and the idea of sexting came into my brain. The idea of a little fore play seemed liked fun before seeing him on the weekend and letting him know that I wanted to take things to next level. So, I texted him back asking if he was thinking about me being there with him on his bed. He picked up on my idea immediately. We had an interesting sexting conversation over the next hour and by the end of that conversation, I think we both needed a cold shower. It was a good thing the weekend was a couple of days away and we would see each other soon enough. My phone rang.

"Hey..."

"What brought that on?"

"I was just thinking about you and this weekend."

"What are you saying?"

"I was thinking that maybe we spend the night together."

"Are you sure?"

"Why wouldn't I be?"

"I just want you to be sure because there's no turning back once we go there."

"I'm sure."

"A'ight. I'll pick you up this weekend. Pack a bag."

"Okay."

I hung up the phone and went to take a shower before I hit the books. My shower was soothing. I came out to find Tee standing there waiting for me in the hallway.

"What's up Tee?"

"We need to talk."

"Uh...okay. What about?"

"Rumor has it that you and Maxwell are getting serious."

"Yeah, kinda...I guess."

"Cool then, have fun this weekend."

"Okay, does everybody know that I'm gonna sleep with him."

"Of course...we are your sisters."

"I hear ya."

Tee smiled and walked back down the hallway and into room. I figured Nia was the one doing the talking, but it really didn't matter as long as it stayed in the house.

The next couple of day passed slowly. It seemed like the weekend would never come around. But Friday finally made its

*way in, and I went about my day going to classes and doing home-
work so that I didn't have to do it over the weekend. Homework or
studying was not about to interrupt my time with Maxwell. I stayed
up late that night finishing it all up. I put the books away and laid
down. I really couldn't sleep, but I closed my eyes and tried. I kept
thinking about spending time with Maxwell and what it would be
like to finally be with him. I think I was starting to make myself sick
by worrying about things. I drifted off to sleep.*

*Darkness entered the room, and I couldn't see anything
around me. From behind me, I heard my name...Nova....Nova. I
looked over my shoulder to my left, but all I could see was blackness. My name was called out again...Nova. I looked over my
shoulder to the right, but again, all I could see was darkness. All of
a sudden, I felt a hand slide down my back as nails scratched into
my skin. A breathe of hot air caused a chill to run up my spine, as I
felt someone breathing next to my ear, then a whisper.*

*"You will always be mine." I could felt the hand slide back
up toward my neck, grabbing my hair, and pulling my head back. I
felt a sharp pain across the left side of my neck. I woke up in a cold
sweat. I looked at my phone to see what time it was. It was 4 am. I
looked over to Nia's bed. She wasn't there. She went out and wasn't
home yet. I laid back down and tried to go back to sleep, but the
dream was so real.*

*The alarm on my phone went off at six. I set it early, so
I could go to the gym and finish up on studying. I got up, got
dressed, and walked over to the gym. I worked out for an hour. I
went to take a shower. I was thinking about the dream. I was also
wondering where Nia was. She didn't come home all night. I got
dressed and walked back through campus to get to the house. It
was a long walk, but I didn't mind because I needed to clear my*

head. As I got back to the house, I saw Nia pulling up in her SUV.

"Hey girl, where ya been?"

"I went out last night. I ran into somebody and you know the rest."

"You crazy."

"Yeah, I'm going to get some sleep. So, it's the big week-end, huh?"

"Not really that big of a deal, but yeah. Imma spend the weekend at Maxwell's."

"Alright girl. I'll talk to you later. I'm tired."

"A'ight."

Nia had already made her way up the stairs and into her bed by the time I got to the room. I laid down as well. I thought I should get some rest before Maxwell picked me up later that day.

I woke up to my text ring tone a couple of hours later. It was Maxwell letting me know that he was going to pick me up sometime around noon. I looked at my clock and it was eleven. I went to wash up. I came back to the room and started to get ready. I was packing some clothes and Nia looked over at me.

"Hey girl. I know I've been a pain in the ass about that boy, but I want you to have fun this weekend."

"A'ight. I hear ya."

"We'll talk when you get back. We'll catch up."

"Yea, I know. See ya when I get back."

I walked out of the room and downstairs. I heard a knock at the door. I opened the door. He stood there, looking down at me, and smiling.

"You ready?"

"Yes."

"Let me have your bag."

*I handed my bag to Maxwell and walked out to his car. He
opened the door for me as he always did, and I got in.*

*"How about we go back to H-Town, have lunch at our
place, do some shopping at the Galleria, and then come home."*

"Sounds like a plan."

*Maxwell smiled at me as he drove us to this family's private
airport. We boarded his plane and took off for Houston. We arrived
forty-five minutes later. A car was waiting for us. To my surprise,
Maxwell had a driver take us around town. We went back to the
same little restaurant to have Jamaican cuisine.*

*We were greeted the by couple who owned it. They told me
they were glad to see me back with Maxwell. I smiled and let them
know that I was happy to be back as well. It appeared that Maxwell had made plans in advance because our food was ready at the
bar. It was the same meal, and it was just as good as I remembered
it the first time. We stayed there for a couple hours and reminisced
about our first date there.*

*We got up to leave for the Galleria, and thanked the couple
again for a wonderful meal.*

*"We'll see you again soon Nova. Mr. Maxwell tells us good
things about you."*

*I was shocked and didn't know what to say to that. I
just looked at them and smiled. Maxwell shook their hands. He
grabbed my hand and we left. The car was waiting for us outside
the restaurant. We got in the backseat and off we went to the Galleria for a day of shopping. I didn't plan on doing any real shopping,
but just some window shopping. We arrived and the driver let us
out at the front entrance.*

*Maxwell and I walked hand in hand. It was nice. We walked
over to the ice skating ring. I stood there and looked at the kids*

skating.

"Do you wanna ice skate?"

"Me...no, I don't know how to ice skate."

"It's a perfect time to learn."

"No, really. I would make a fool outta myself."

"I'll teach you. I won't let you fall. Promise."

"I'm not sure, and I know there's a first time for everything, but let's do it another time."

"A'ight."

We left and started to walk around. There were so many stores, but the shoes stores are what caught my interest. Max- well wanted to buy me something, but I refused. I didn't want him thinking that was the purpose of me being with him. I'm sure some people thought that was the reason I was dating him.

"Let's have a drink."

"Okay."

We went over to this Mexican restaurant in the food court. We sat on the patio which was still located inside the Galleria. Maxwell asked what I would like to drink.

"A margarita on the rocks please."

"I'll be right back, it's taking too long for the waiter to come over. I'll go order it at the bar."

"Okay."

He went over to get the drinks and brought them back.

"Here you go."

"Wow...it's strong. Are you trying to get me drunk?"

"Of course. I'm joking...do you want me to get you another that's not as strong."

"No, it's okay. I'm good."

We sat there, talked and drank. I was looking around at all the people passing by. I like Houston, but it just wasn't home. It was a nice little get-a-way when you needed that. The waiter came over and asked if we needed another drink. Maxwell asked me if I wanted another. I agreed to another. We continued to talk about things, but neither of us brought up the subject of tonight. The waiter brought back our drinks. We carried on our conversation while finishing up our drinks. Maxwell asked if I wanted another drink or if I was ready to go home.

"I'm ready to go home Maxwell. It's was a nice day. Thank you."

Maxwell called the waiter over and signed for the bill. We got up and walked to the front of the Galleria and out the exit. The car was waiting for us. I never understood how the drivers knew that we were ready to go, but they were always waiting on us. Maxwell opened the door for me. I got in. As he was getting in, he remembered he left his card at the bar in the Mexican restaurant.

"I'll be right back Nova. Sorry."

"It's okay. No big deal."

"I know how you don't like me running out on you."

"Funny, Maxwell, funny."

Maxwell ran back inside. It took him about twenty minutes to get back to the car. He opened the door and got in.

"My bad. They couldn't find my card."

"It's okay."

The driver drove us back to the airport. We boarded the plane and arrived back home within an hour. Maxwell's car was waiting as we arrived. He grabbed his keys out of his pocket, and made his way over to the passenger door to open it for me. I was starting to get use to him doing things for me like that. I got in, and he closed the door. He walked around to the driver side and got in.

We drove off. We arrived at his home. We got out of his car, and he opened his trunk to get my bag out. He walked me inside.

"Are you okay with staying the night?"

"Yes, I told you that I am."

"Just making sure Nova."

"I know Maxwell."

He walked over to the bar, poured me a glass of wine, and handed it to me. I smiled at him and took the glass. He turned on some music. I asked him if anyone was home besides us. I didn't want any surprises like the last time I stayed over.

"No...it's just you and me tonight. And I promise I will be here in the morning."

"I hear ya."

We walked over to one of the dining areas. We sat down. I was drinking my wine as he took the glass from me. He put it on one of the end tables. I looked at him. He came closer to me and slid his hand through my hair and down to the back of my neck. He pulled me toward him and started kissing me. As with each time before, a sensation ripped through my body as his lips pressed against mine. It started out soft and sensual, but then we started kissing hard.

Maxwell's hand slid from the back of my neck and down my backside. His hand moved onto my leg as he caressed it, and made its way back up toward the inside of my thigh. His lips made their way toward my neck as he kissed it gently. My eyes were closed and my head was titled back.

"Let's go upstairs Nova."

I opened my eyes and looked at him. There was no refusing him from this point. He grabbed my hand and led me up to his room. As we got there, I walked toward his bed. He walked over to *me and we started to kiss again. I got onto his bed and laid back. He laid next to me and started to unbutton my shirt. His hands moved down to my jeans. He kept kissing me while he was un-clothing me. His touch was so soft. He looked at me. I pulled his shirt off over his head. My hands slide down his abs and onto his jeans. I unfastened them. The moment had finally arrived as I felt his presence taking over mine. I was enjoying every minute of the experience and then blackness came over me.*

I awoke the next morning in his arms. It would have been the greatest feeling in the world if I had not felt several burning sensations on my back and stomach. The burning sensations felt dull though compared to the pain I felt on the left side of my neck. I took my hand and reached up to my neck to rub it. Maxwell looked over at me.

"Hey, are you okay?"

"Yeah, what do you mean?"

"You passed out last night."

I was trying to think, but my head wasn't clear. I knew that Maxwell and I slept together, but I couldn't remember the entire night.

"I know this may sound bad, but did I pass out before or after?"

"Wow...that's not good for my ego."

"I'm sorry."

"It's alright Nova."

I got up to use the bathroom. On my way, I noticed in the mirror that I had several scratch mark on my stomach. I turned around and had several on back. My neck was still in pain. I took a closer in the mirror. It looked as if something bit me, maybe a spider or something.

I came out and laid back down next to Maxwell. He put his arm around me. I looked up at him and smiled.

"We should get up."

"Okay then."

Maxwell got up and went into the bathroom. I got up and got dressed. He came out of the restroom.

"Well, let's see what we can do about breakfast."

"A'ight."

We went downstairs and into the kitchen.

"I make a mean omelet. Is that cool Nova?"

"Yeah, that's good. I'm not really hungry though."

"Hmm...then maybe we'll wait and have lunch."

"Sounds like a plan."

We both smiled. Maxwell walked over to me and put his arms around me. He whispered in my ear that he had no regrets about last night. I had no clue what he meant, but I whispered back I didn't either.

We spent the rest day of the day just hanging out at his place. It was getting late and I had to get back to the house. I needed to be in class first thing in the morning. Actually, I needed to be in every class because finals were around the corner and I had to ace them. Maxwell drove me home. We said our good nights and he kissed me.

"Nova, I have something for you."

"What?"

"I picked you something up in Houston."

"Why? I told you I didn't want you to buy me anything."

"I know, but I saw it when we were window shopping, and so, I went back in to get it when I told you I left my card at the restaurant."

"So, you lied to me?"

"It was for a good cause. I hope you like it. Open it before you go to bed tonight."

"Okay. Thanks."

"I'll call you tomorrow."

I said ok, closed his car door, and walked inside.

I walked in and all the girls were sitting in the common area. They tried to act like they were doing something but I knew they were waiting on me.

"Hey Nova, we almost forgot you weren't here."

"Whatever Nia."

"So...how was it girl?"

"Ugh! AJ it's rude to ask her that."

"Whatever Jules, you know you're curious as well."

"Yeah, she is."

"Whatever, Em...you know you wanna know too."

"Look, it was good. That's all I will say. So...Good night ya'll."

"Oh no you don't think you're going to leave it like that."

"Yeah, I do Nia."

"Alright, ya'll leave her alone."

"Why you taking up for her Tee?"

"Uh, don't worry about it. Just let it be."

"Yeah, Yeah."

I walked up to my room and laid down. I looked at the box he gave me. I was so curious about what it was. I couldn't resist waiting any longer, so I opened it. It was a bracelet. It was beautiful. It had an antique silver finishing and a huge pearl in the middle of it. I'd never seen anything quite like it, but it was definitely something I would buy for myself. My eyes closed and I was thinking about the weekend, and soon enough I was off dreaming.

My alarm woke me up that next morning. I got up, and did the usual routine. I went to all my classes. The day went by quickly as did the night. I was lying down to go to bed before I knew it. I didn't get a call or text from Maxwell. I wonder what was going on, but I didn't contact him. I fell asleep that night with him on my mind again. I woke up the next morning to find he was still on my mind. I couldn't recall any dreams I had during the night which meant my mind must have been preoccupied.

A couple days passed and still no word from Maxwell. I started to think I had made a huge mistake. The week passed by slowly, but Friday rolled around and he text me. He apologized for not hitting me up during the week because he was busy. I replied as I always did when I feel like I need to be on my guard by saying 'it was all good'. He asked me if I was going out. I told him I was going out with my girls. He replied by saying cool and that he would hit me up later then. I found no reason to reply back to him.

I got back to the house and went up to my room. Nia was sitting at the computer.

"Hey girl, lets hit a new spot tonight."

"A'ight. Cool."

I sat down, but closed my eyes to give them a rest. I was tired from the week. My mind was off in another world before I knew it. Nia woke me up not too long after I fell asleep and before I could have any dreams.

"Hey girl, get up and get ready."

"OMG! What time is it?"

"It's like seven, but you know how long it takes you."

"A'ight."

I got ready. It was going to be just Nia and I that night be-

*cause everybody else had plans or dates. We went out to Northeast
side of town, and ended up in an Ultra Lounge inside the loop off
of Broadway. It was a nice place, and had a cool atmosphere about
it. The scenery was especially nice as there were a lot of good
looking guys in the place. It was already crowded by the time we
got there. We ordered a drink and walked around to check things
out. We made our way over by the dance floor and just chilled
there. Nia couldn't resist but to talk to every guy that passed us by.
It seemed like old times when we first met. We were both laughing,
sharing our opinions about what people shouldn't be wearing, and
looking for possible potentials as we made our way out to dance in
the middle of the dance floor.*

> *"Hey girl, I seriously need another drink."*
> *"Alright. Let's go get one."*

*We walked over to the bar. I was trying to get the bartender's atten-
tion. Nia shoved me on my shoulder.*

> *"What's up?"*
> *"Look."*

> *She made a tossing suggestion with her head for me to look*
*toward the door. Maxwell was making his way through the door
with some chick on his arm.*

> *"Leave it alone girl."*
> *"Uh-uuh...please tell me that you're not going to put up*
with that crap?"
> *"Yeah, it's all good."*
> *"No way Nova...if you don't go say something I will."*
> *I looked at her and told her to forget about it. She couldn't*
*understand why I wasn't going to call him out and bust him. I
ordered our drinks and we went back out to the dance floor. We
danced all night. I didn't look for Maxwell and I didn't know if he*

saw me there. If he did, he never brought it up to me.

The semester ended and summer vacation rolled around. Maxwell and I continued to talk, but we really didn't hang out as much. We'd get together every now and then, but it wasn't like it was before. Nia hated him even more than she did before. She told me I shouldn't talk to him again, but I still felt some type of attachment to him. It was unexplainable.

We all hung out over the summer break. We went out on a regular basis and hung out in some of the local bars. But it was Nia and I who spent a lot time hanging around and getting into trouble. The summer seemed to pass by as fast as it rolled in. The fall the semester would soon arrive, and we'd be back to class.

Nia and I went out one week night, and we ran into Maxwell again. He was with another girl. I was drunk and had a falling out with him. Nia told me he wasn't worth the trouble. That weekend we headed to Corpus Christi, Texas for some fun.

CHAPTER NINE

As I was about to log off of Hookup.com, something caught my attention. Something as in someone caught my attention. The subject line of the message I received contained one word. The word was 'Hey'. I looked at the profile picture, but it was blurred, and he was standing at a distance. He appeared to be tall, but that was all I really could tell from the picture.

I opened his message, and read it. It was simple, but different. It wasn't about hooking up with him at all. He was starting a conversation, and what appeared to me as trying to find out who I was. He asked me if I was originally from San Antonio, and what I was doing on the site, and what I was seeking from it, but what really caught my attention was the question in which he asked how my day was going. In all the messages I read and replied to, not one other guy asked that. I found that very intriguing, and found myself replying back to him even though I couldn't get a visual of what he looked like.

As I sent my reply off to him, I noticed he went offline, so I decided to do the same since I had to get to sleep to attend class in the morning.....

"Hey chica, miss me? I see not since your giving up on finding me."

"Nia where the hell are you? I hear you, but I can't see. Stop playin'."

She laughed with her unique giggle, and I recalled the first time I ever heard it.

"I'm right here...can't you see me?"

I turned in every direction and all I could see was darkness.

"Dammit Nia, don't do this to me."

"Your giving up on me...you all are. You're living your lives, moving on as I'm becoming a faded memory. I expect it from them Nova, but not you."

As she said those words, I felt the coldness enter the room with us. That same coldness every time I heard that snarling voice call out my name.

"Nova!"

"Nia, where are you?"

I put my hands out in front of me to feel around, but I couldn't find her.

"Nova...Nova...you know she will only do for the time being."

"NO! Nia run...run!"

"Nova, help me....No, get away!"

In the background, I hear Nia screaming the suddenly I feel a claw like hand grab my neck and pull me toward whatever it was in front of me. I could feel the hot breath of air rush up against my face coming from it's nose and mouth. As it snarled with every word it spoke.

"It won't stop with her. There will be others unless you give me what I want."

"What do you want? Why are you doing this?"

"You Nova, just you...as we have been destined to be together since the day we were born on this earth...I shall not stop until I get what I want."

I could feel him right in front of my face even though I

couldn't see him. I turned my face as he drew closer. I felt his
sharp nails dig into my throat and felt some of my blood drip down
from his grasp. He snarled, and I could hear the grin appear as he
licked the blood from my throat. I tried to push him away, but he
was too strong. I kept hearing Nia in the background screaming,
and calling out my name.

All of a sudden, a light appeared. AJ was standing in front
of me and calling out my name. I looked at her, and then looked
around.

"Are you okay Nova? What are you doing sitting up in the
dark?"

I was sitting down on my bed with my eyes wide open
when she turned on the light as she entered the room. This was unlike any of the other times that I dreamed of this being in the cold
darkness. I didn't understand it. How could I be dreaming if I was
wide awake?

"Nova, are you okay?"

"Yes, I'm okay."

"What time is it?"

"It's a lil' after 5 a.m., and I was just checking if you were
gonna go to the gym before classes."

"I'm not in the mood today."

"You haven't been in the mood to do anything but be
online. You haven't gone to class since Nia went missing. You
haven't gone out. I know you miss Nia, and we all do too, but you
can't stop living."

"O' my gosh! AJ, how can you stand there, and say that?
Nia's missing, and you want me to forget about that? Just go on
with my life and enjoy it while she could be fighting for her life
somewhere. What happen to us searching for her and trying to find

out who the mystery man is that she had that date with?"

"Nova, we are all still trying to find out, but we understand that it can't consume our lives either. Nia wouldn't want us to stop living."

"What do you know about what Nia wants? Nia would want us to find her!"

"You're obsessed! We all are stilling doing our part. Luna has been talking to the person she is looking into. So have I…so have all our sisters. We have not given up, but we are still doing other things to help us cope through this situation. You have to do the same."

"You cope with it your way, and I'll cope with it my way. And FYI, I had already planned to go to classes today."

"Fine."

AJ stormed out of the room, as I was about to apologize for going off on her. She was so mad at me that she didn't even close the door or look back at me. She could carry quite an attitude if anyone pushed her to it, but she never reacted on it. In a way, I knew she was right, and she was just worried about me, but I kept thinking about seeing Nia. I sat there for a minute in thought, as I tried to replay what I saw in my vision of Nia. I wouldn't give up on finding her or finding the mystery man behind her disappearance. I got up, grabbed a t-shirt, jeans, panties, bra, and headed over to shower and change. I left the sorority house, and headed over to the campus for my classes.

As I walked into the building, I glanced over at someone walking out. For a brief minute, I swear I saw her, but I knew it was impossible. I walked in the door, and up the stairs to head over to the lecture room for my political science class. I was a junior and taking a freshman semester course, but since I didn't declare my major until the end of my sophomore year, I had no choice in the matter.

"Yo, where's your girl at? I haven't heard her mouth or seen her in my face in a while."

I turned around, and walked over to him.

"What the fuck did you say! Did you have anything to do with it Maxwell? Did you?"

"Don't come at me like that Nova…what the hell are you talking about? Anything to do with what?"

"Don't play stupid with me. Nia's missing. The whole freakin' campus knows and you're telling me you haven't heard about it."

"Uh, no…I guess I'm not the only one that doesn't keep up with what's going on. In case you haven't realized, I've been out of town for a lil' while."

"When did you leave?"

"Right after we last talked."

"You mean the night you called and told me we couldn't be friends?"

"Yeah, Nova, that night."

"Well, I didn't know."

"Look, can we talk?"

"Naw, there ain't nothing' to talk about."

"I see by the change in your tone and accent you are still upset."

"It's all good."

He laughed, as he shook his head and looked at me.

"Ms. Salinas there's no need for you to get your guard up with me. I just wanted a couple of minutes of your time."

"Maxwell, what do you want? You said everything you

need to say that night. What more do you need to say? I gotta get
to class."

"Yeah, you do. I haven't seen you on campus either lately,
and been asking around for you."

"Yeah, whateva...Imma be late."

"Have lunch with me?"
I laughed sarcastically under my breath.

"Lunch with you? I would have to be outta my mind."

"We already know that, so what time is your last morning
class?"

"Sorry, not this time...not this easy. See ya 'round."

I walked off, didn't look back at him, and walked into the
lecture hall. It was the only class I didn't really know anyone who
I talked to or hung out with as most of the student body in there
were under classmen. So, I picked out the cutest guy in class, and
went over to sit by him. It was the start of something I set out in
motion, and yet had no idea what a huge monster I would be creating. I introduced myself, and started a conversation with him. Half
way through it, I started flirting and flashing my smile, and before
class was over, I not only had his name and number, but I had
plans to meet him down in the Sombrilla area for lunch. I knew
Maxwell would be there waiting on me to show, but he had no idea
that I wouldn't be alone.

I carried on with my morning and went to my remaining
two classes for the day. After my last class, I walked over to the
cafeteria, and met up with my lunch date. I wasn't really hungry,
but I ordered anyway, and we went outside to grab a table to eat
and talk. He was actually a funny guy, and had me laughing so
hard, I didn't see Maxwell walk up.

"Hey."

"What's up?"

"Friend of yours?" my lunch date asked.

"Nope, just an acquaintance."

"Funny, you got a minute?"

"Doesn't look like I do at the moment. But, I'm sure you can find someone else who does have a minute for you. You're quite good at that."

"A'ight...cool."

"See ya 'round...maybe."

I apologized for the interruption and continued talking. We stayed at the table for a couple hours and just talked about anything and nothing. Next thing we knew, we were headed back to his dorm room. I wasn't really into him, but he was a good looking guy, funny, and I was looking for a quick way to get over Maxwell. The sex was good and intense, and over rather quickly. I got up, got dressed, and asked him to do the same. He walked me downstairs, and out the door. I hugged him, and said good-bye. I never talked to him again, and avoided him altogether for the rest of the semester.

As I walked back through campus and headed back to the sorority house, I heard Jules laughing.

"Wow! You wanna let everyone in the dorm know what you were up to?"

I looked at her and just grinned.

"My bad, I didn't know anyone was checking up on me."

"Naw, I wasn't checking up on you, I just happened to be around , but damn, seems like you took out a lotta frustration out on that poor guy."

"Was it that obvious I haven't had sex in a while?"

"I don't know. I was talking about you getting the hell up

outta there as soon you got what you needed. Whatever happened to cuddling after?"

"You crack me up Jules, why the hell would I want to talk or cuddle when I already got what I needed?"

"I see…you run into Maxwell because he's been looking for you?"

"How you know?"

"He stopped me in the courtyard a couple of days ago, and asked about you."

"Well, he found me today, but I'm not ready to listen to the same bullshit again."

"A'ight girl…those are your issues, but for the record, he seemed genuinely concerned about you. Just saying."

"Yeah, so he tried to tell me."

I walked upstairs, as we arrived at the house, and laid down on my bed. I fell asleep and woke up without recalling one dream in that quick nap. It was the best feeling in the world, to have my mind completely shut down instead of it racing a hundred miles per hour. I attributed that feeling with the sex I just had with someone I didn't give a damn about.

I immediately jumped online to Hookup.com, and started several conversations, with several guys, that lasted through the night. By the time I headed off to dreamland, I had confirmed dates, and there wasn't one night I didn't have any plans booked. Before I logged off, I noticed a reply from the guy who caught my interest the first night I created my profile. I looked at it, but I didn't open it. He was too intriguing in his own unique way, and I didn't want to get caught up in something that would lead to emotions. I just had some strange feeling about him, and was trusting my instincts to stay away from him and his message. I was in my own world for the time being, and enjoying the feeling of not feeling anything at all. It looked good on me, and being selfish was about to become one of my strong points.

My routine became like clockwise day in and night out. Monday through Thursday, I attend class in morning, then eat lunch on most days, get back to the house before any of the girls would get there, go online, study for a few hours, get dressed, and then be off to meet a new guy. Friday, Saturday, and Sunday, I'd sleep in late, get online and meet new people, talk to the guys who I had a set date with for that night, maybe set up an earlier date with some other guy if I talked to someone interesting enough, and then stay out until the morning hours. My sorority sisters were seeing less and less of me as I was starting to detach myself from them and anyone else I cared about.

Every night out became the same ritual. I meet a new guy for drinks at a familiar place to me. We laugh, talk, dance, and drink. And most nights, I'd walk out of a place and head over to his place. Now and then, my instincts would kick in and get a bad feeling about a guy, and I would just end the night early. I don't know if it was coincidence or not, but the nights I ended on an early note, those were nights the dreams became intensely darker, and I saw Nia each and every time.

My visions or dream, at the time I didn't really know what to call them, ended in the same manner but with each of them, it got darker and colder. I would find myself after each occurrence with bruises, cuts, and deep scratches that I couldn't explain how I received them. All I would remember was having the feeling of fighting someone off me or feeling pinned down, and hearing that voice. I tried to make those nights disappear quickly as I made sure I wouldn't have early nights. I'd basically throw myself into meaningless sex to avoid any occurrences with whatever was afflicting the injuries upon me, but after several tries of not being alone, the worst happened.

It was a typical Saturday night, and I was getting ready to meet a new guy I just met online. We chatted several times over the week and made plans to meet. From our conversations, I concluded he seemed pretty cool. I wasn't too excited about meeting him, as I knew it would probably turn out like all the other dates. In the process of waiting for my flat iron to heat up, I decided to jump online. I was surprised when I saw a message from Brackz as I had not heard from him in a week or maybe more. I opened his email and read through it. His words were still breathtaking, and even though he was roughly the same age, he appeared to be much older. I just assumed it was a cultural thing. I replied back immediately, as did he. An hour had passed and I finally told him I had to end the conversation for the night. He replied and asked me not to end the night with him. I emailed him back to let him know I had set plans for the night. His reply seems to suggest he was irritated with my response. He asked me to jump onto the IM, so we could chat just a little more before I left for the night. I replied with an "I'm sorry, but I really have to go for now". He replied back, but I did not open it and logged off of my email account.

I logged onto Hookup.com, and looked at my messages. I don't know why, but I kept looking at the message I never opened from the guy who caught my interest that first night on the site. I sat there for a minute, and I asked myself why I was so afraid to read his message. I had no clue. Maybe it had to do with the fact that it took him so little work to capture my attention. Next thing I know, my curiosity got the best of me, and I was opening his message. I was stunned and laughing at the same time. His message read:

Hey Ma,

I'm not the usual guy on here, and I'm sure you heard that before, but I'm quite different. I know you probably get a lot of messages from people on the site trying to get in your pants, but I have a feeling that's not what your really about. For me, a female needs to be able to hold a conversation with me first and foremost, and then keep my interest before I decide if she's worth getting my attention. So, if you think you fit the profile, and you think you can hold a conversation with me, then let's talk. If not, thanks for your response and time.

I was intrigued at that point. It was the first time a guy told me point blank I had to get and keep his interest if I wanted to know him. I was used to guys trying to get my interest, and yet, when they did, they never kept it very long. I smiled at the computer screen and logged off. I kept thinking to myself, this guy has to be damned arrogant or that damned confident. There's a fine line between a man being arrogant or being confident, and confidence was damn sexy in my book, but regardless I wasn't going to respond immediately and let him know that I was that interested in getting to know the person behind the message.

I finished up, getting ready and headed out for the night. I chose a strange place to go, and had no idea why, but ended up meeting my date at the club where I first met NC Kidd, aka Maxwell. It was early, so the place was still empty. I walked over to the bar and proceeded to order a hurricane. He walked over, and introduced himself.

"Hello Nova"

"Hey there, glad you found the place."

"Yes, I've actually been here a couple of times."

"Cool. Hope you weren't waiting too long, but I got caught up in some things."

"No problem. I was actually surprised you agreed to meet me tonight."

"Why?"

"Well, I'm kinda new to this online dating thing."
I laughed and then smiled.

"I see. So, I get to break you in tonight, huh?"
He laughed.

"That's funny. I think that's what got my attention about you Nova. You have a great sense of humor."

"Thanks George."

"No need to thank me. I'm just telling the truth."

We both sat down at the bar and continued our conversation. The night was going good, and he was funny as well. We continued to order drinks, as we enjoyed each other's company. It was getting later in the night, and I knew that by the all the people entering the place. Before we knew it, it was a packed house. He asked me if I wanted to leave and go somewhere else less crowded so we could continue the great conversation we were having. I agreed, but had to use the restroom, and asked him to wait for me.

I headed down toward the restroom, as I fought my way through the crowd. As I was nearing the entrance to the hall that led to the restrooms, a hand grabbed me by my arm. I was startled by that touch.

"What's wrong...why so jumpy?"
I turned to look at him.

"Hey...I just didn't expect that."

"You here with your girls?"

"Naw, not tonight."

"Oh ok, maybe I should let you get back to whatever."

"How you been?"

"As good as could be Nova."

"Yeah, I hear ya Maxwell."

He smiled, and I turned back and headed toward the ladies room. I laughed as I entered. I saw the same female that was with Maxwell the night we had the falling out at the club. She sarcastically smiled at me. I just shook my head, and walked passed her.

"Yo, you need to stay away from my man."

I walked into one of the stalls without turning around or saying anything.

"I know you heard me bitch."

I just thought to myself, "Nova, it's not worth it, so don't let her get to you". I proceeded to walk back out of the stall, and over to the sink to wash my hands.

"I'm still right here…did you fuckin' hear me?"

I looked at her through the mirror,

"Look girl, whatever you think it is that you're doing…it's not gonna work. If you have an insecurity issue about Maxwell and me, then that's on you. I don't want your man."

"Keep it that way or Imma fuck you up."

I laughed and continue to shake my head. I walked out of the restroom and was making my way back over to George. When he walked up behind me. His placed his hand next to my neck and pulled my hair back from my ear. He whispered, "I miss you". I looked over my shoulder, and just starred at him. I was upset with him that he said that. I grabbed his hand and removed it.

"Not now…don't do this now."

"I can't help but to do it now because you won't give me a

chance to explain things."

"There's nothing to explain. By the way, your girl just had some interesting words for me."

"What girl?"

"C'mon Maxwell, your girl…the girl you always hanging with these days."

"She's not my girl…The only person I ever called my girl is standing right here next to me."

"I think you had a little too much to drink tonight."

"By the looks of it, you're the one who had too much. Let me drive you home."

"Uh, no. I'm not here by myself."

"But you did drive here by yourself."

"If you say so. Good night Maxwell."

I walked away from him and back over to George who was watching from a far intensely.

"A'ight, I'm ready. Let's head out."

"Is everything okay?"

"Yeah, why you ask?"

"Well, your friend is still looking this way, and he's not smiling."

"Don't worry about him. He'll be ok. Let's go."

George and I walked out of the club and down the street to a small place. It was a pub, and the music was going. There weren't many people in the place, but it had a cool atmosphere to it. It was the first time I had been there. I sat at one of the tables as he went to order us a drink. We sat there, talked, and laughed for the next hour until it was last call.

"You ready Nova?"

"Yeah, I think I'm good for the night."

"I'll walk you to your car."

"Thanks. I'd like that. Your okay George."

He laughed.

"You too."

We said good night to the bartender, and walked outside, and down to the parking garage.

"I'm on the 5th floor I think."

"Okay, let's take the elevator."

The ring of the elevator sounded, and the doors opened. We walked in, the doors closed behind us, and then he got really close to me. I looked up at him as he was over six feet tall. He smiled at me, and then kissed me. I closed my eyes as I felt his lips pressed against mine. I could feel the smile on my face as we kissed. I don't know if it was the sensation of the kiss or if it was the amount of drink I had, but I was feeling pretty light-headed. The doors opened and it was dark. The lights on the 5th floor were completely out. I reached for my cell phone for some light to see in front of me.

"Hey, stay close to me."

"I'm not afraid of the dark George."

"I didn't say you were, but these light's shouldn't be out."

I laughed.

"Where's your car at?" It was right around the corner from the elevator.

"Is that it?"

"Yep, that's me."

"Very nice."

"Thanks."

He grabbed my hand and pulled me toward him. Even though, I couldn't see anything, I closed my eyes.

* * * * * * *

I opened my eyes, and looked around. I couldn't recall how I got into my bed or for that matter how I got back to the sorority house. I couldn't remember saying bye to George, getting in my car, or driving back. I looked at my cell phone, and saw a missed text. I immediately thought it had to be George. I put my phone down without viewing the message, and went to the bathroom. I came back to my room, and opened my phone. It was from Maxwell. He was asking if he could see me that day, so we could talk about things. I decided not reply until I thought about how I was going to respond.

I walked over to the computer. I logged into my email. I opened Brackz's message. In his message, he told me to have a good time, and said he wanted to ask me something important. I looked at the email weird because I didn't know what was so important that he needed to ask me. I replied to him saying "to ask". I switched to another screen, and logged onto Hookup.com. There were so many messages, but I only had one on my mind that I was interested in replying back to. I opened it, and hit the reply button:

Hey there,

Well that was a interesting read. Since you have my attention, let's see how long you can keep it…O' wait, that was your line. LOL.

I hit the send button, and off my reply went. As I was about to open some of the other messages, I noticed he replied immediately. Our messages went back and forth, and we were both very sarcastic in our responses. It was unusual to talk to someone who had a good sense of humor and a similar sarcasm about them as I did. I wondered if I was still asleep and dreaming because I didn't think it could be possible to meet two very cool guys on a site such as this one.

I noticed my email had a new mail, so I clicked back over to that screen. It was from Brackz.

Hey Sexy,

How did your night go? Well, there is something I wanted to talk to you about. I've been thinking about you a lot, and even though we stopped messaging for a minute, I can't help but think I would be a fool to let an opportunity pass me by to meet you if I could. We get along so great, and I feel like I already know you. I'm doing some work in the States, and I don't know exactly how close Texas is to New York, even if it's not, I would like the chance to meet you in person. So, my question to you is: Do you want to meet me?

I was actually shocked, not that he wanted to meet me, but that he would be willing to come all this way to do so. I didn't know what to say or how to reply. There were so many things going on at the moment. I was dealing with Maxwell, George, the new guy who was quite intriguing, and now Brackz. My head was spinning, so I got up and walked back over to my bed. I sat down, I grabbed my cell, and replied to Maxwell's text. I told him I would meet him on one condition, and that was we meet for an early dinner, in town, and no drinks. He replied back immediately, and agreed. We set a time for 6 o'clock at one of my favorite spots to eat. My phone rang…

"Hey, thanks for meeting me tonight."

"You're welcome."

"How about I just pick you up, so you don't have to drive there."

"No. I'll meet you there."

"Ok Nova. I'll see you at 6."

"Bye Maxwell."

I hung up the phone. I looked over at the computer, and went back to take care of the other question asked of me. I went back into my email, and responded to Brackz. I told him I would be okay with meeting him for dinner and drinks, and I just needed to know which day would be good for him.

I switched back over to the other screen, and continued my conversation with the new guy I met online. We sent messages back and forth for about an hour, but it wasn't quite the same with him. He was asking questions, but they weren't the routine "let's get to know each other" questions. He went about it a different way, and I liked that because I was so tired of answering the same old questions that everyone else was asking me. I asked about him and where he was from. He let me know he didn't consider himself from any one place because he had moved so much, so he didn't call any place home. He went on to say that he was born in Texas but soon after his parents moved. I asked him what brought him to S.A. He replied, his field of work, but didn't know how long that would keep him around.

As we kept talking via messages, I felt like I knew him from somewhere. Several hours had passed, and before I logged off to get ready to meet Maxwell, I realized we hadn't exchanged names. I think we both realized it at the same time because as I sent him a message to ask his name, I received a message from him asking mine. I laughed as I replied "Nova", as I received his reply saying Anenthen. He sent another message instantly, asking for my number, and if it was okay to text me. I replied with my number, and told him to find out.

As I logged off my computer, my text ring tone sounded. I went over to pick up my cell. It was a number I didn't recognize, but the text read: U tell me. I shook my head, smiled, and replied: I guess this is your way of giving me your number. He responded: Guess it's okay to text after all, huh? Lol. I didn't respond back, but I had the feeling he knew he would definitely hear from me again.

* * * * * * *

I walked over to the table where Maxwell was sitting. He got up, pulled out my seat for me, then sat back down.

"I hope you don't mind, but I already placed our order."

"Really? And how do you know what I wanted?" He smiled at me.

"Because Ms. Salinas, you order the same thing every time we came here."
I tried to look annoyed and tried to stop the smile from appearing on my face.

"Well, maybe I have an appetite for something new."

"Maybe. If you want something else, I can order it for you." I rolled my eyes, and looked over to the couple sitting next to us.

"Sure, I would like…" I proceeded to order something else off the menu, but I knew what I really wanted was exactly what he ordered me.

"Okay, I'll get that for you."

"No, wait. What you ordered is fine."

"I know Ms. Salinas."

Maxwell and I just sat there for a couple of minutes without saying anything and just looked at each other. We started to talk about what was going on recently, and how each of us was doing. Our food finally arrived to the table. We kept talking while we ate. A couple of hours had passed, and it seemed like old times as if nothing bad happened between us that passed year.

Maxwell asked me how my family was doing, and also asked about Nia. I told him my mom and the rest of the family were doing fine. I looked down at the table as I responded to him about Nia because I knew that my behavior the last couple of weeks was so selfish that I couldn't look him in his eyes to tell him that I didn't know about Nia, her whereabouts, or if she was even alive. Tears ran down my eyes, as I placed my elbows on the table, and laid my head in my hands to cover my face. He pulled me over next to him, and told me it would be okay.

"Let's get outta here Nova."

"Sure."

We walked over to his car, and he opened the door for me. I got in his BMW, buckled up, and he closed the door. We drove to downtown, and to the parking garage that I was at the night before kissing George. It was blocked off with yellow tape. He pulled up, rolled down his window, and asked the attendant if there was parking available.

"Not tonight, Sir."

"How can you not have any parking this early?"

"We apologize for any inconvenience, but a man was killed here last night on the 5th floor, and police have blocked off the entire parking garage.

"Excuse me, you said someone was killed here last night on

the 5th floor?"

"Yes, ma'am. Early this morning rather, after the clubs closed. You can park a block down, there should be plenty of availability since it's still early."

"Thank you."

I looked at Maxwell.

"What is it?"

"I was on the 5th floor last night. It was after the club closed, it was dark."

"Please don't tell me that dude let you walk to your car alone."

"No, he walked me, but all I remember is him walking me to my car. I woke up this morning, and I don't know how I got home...I don't remember anything after getting off the elevator and walking over to my car."

"Let's just be thankful you're okay."

"Yeah, I guess. I've never blacked out like that before though."

"Excuse me, I recall one time in particular that you can't remember." He laughed.

"You had to bring that up." I was shaking my head and smiling.

We drove over to the next parking lot, parked, and walked over to the club. We only had two drinks while we continued our conversation. Maxwell wanted to get into his explanation of why he did what he did, but I wouldn't allow him to go there. I told him we could discuss it later, but tonight I just wanted to hang out and have some laughs. He agreed to it. We left that night as friends, and he drove me back over to the restaurant to pick up my car, and then he followed me back to the sorority house to make sure I got home safely.

CHAPTER TEN

I was standing next to my car, looking for the right button on the remote to open the door. I felt his hand on my back, and him asking me if I needed help.

"No...I'm fine. I don't need help pushing a button George."
He laughed.

"Apparently you do Nova."
As I turned around to feel where he was at. I didn't feel him behind me anymore.

"George?" He didn't answer.

"Hey, not funny. George?"
My heart started beating fast as I felt a cold shiver come across me. I reached for my cell phone, but dropped it on the floor along with my keys. I kept calling out for him, but he wasn't responding to me calling out. I dropped to the floor to find my cell or my keys. I heard something coming from behind me. I started to panic.

"RAWWRRR" He laughed.

"Dammit!! That wasn't funny!"

"I'm sorry Nova"

"You're stupid...don't ever do that shit again. I could have hurt you."

"Yeah, right. You were so scared. I'm sorry, I shouldn't have done that, but I couldn't resist."

"I hate you."

"No, you don't."

I was mad and still on the ground looking for the keys.
George and I both reached out at the same time and found them.
He pulled me up, and then he hugged me.

It was still so dark, and I couldn't see anything but I felt
him right in front of me. He leaned in to kiss me again. As we
kissed, I felt him drop to the floor. The kissing got passionate, and
then I felt my hand reach up, and with all my might, slung it toward
his neck as my nail gashed into his flesh. I felt the splatter of warm
blood against my skin. I grinned.

I was shaking and in a cold sweat when I came to. I was
sitting on my bed. I wasn't sure if I was dreaming or if what I just
saw was a memory of what happened the night before on the date
with George. It was so real like that I couldn't go back to sleep. I
realized I hadn't heard from George since that night. I kept thinking it had to be a dream, and I decided to call him to put my mind
at ease. I dialed his number, and it rang, and rang, and rang, but
there was no answer. My imagination was starting to get the best
of me. Why couldn't I remember what happened that night after
we got off the elevator? I got up and went over to the computer. I
started a search for the killing that happened that night.

My heart dropped when I read the news story report. The
identity of the man killed in the parking garage was released with
a photo. At first, I couldn't find anything on it, but then I came
across the website for one of the local news stations. I didn't know
George's full name, but there his photo was, and investigator
had no leads. I couldn't explain how police didn't have any leads
because George and I went to a very well know establishment, and
the other was so small that the bartender had to remember us. The
parking garage had camera surveillance, so I was sure that I was

captured on tape with him. I thought to myself, "Why haven't the police contacted me for questioning". My mind was racing a hundred miles an hour again. Did I dream the entire thing up?

My text ring tone went off. I jumped at the sound of it. It was Anenthen. He was texting to find out how my day was going, and if I would be available to meet him for dinner or a movie that night. I couldn't think about going out at the moment, so I didn't respond. The door to my room opened, and all the girls were standing there.

"What?"

The all entered the room and surrounded me as I sat at the computer. I turned the screen off.

"Well?"

"Nova, we need to talk to you."

"So talk Tee."

"We're worried about you. You haven't been around lately, nor do you hang out with us or even talk to us anymore. It's like you're avoiding us."

"Tee, I just need some time to myself. There's so much going on."

"I'm about to meet Brackz, and I've been talking to Maxwell again."

"Maxwell?"

"Yeah, I didn't tell y'all this but Maxwell is one of the guys on Nia's person's list who she last added before she disappeared. AJ is the only other person who knows."

"Why you keeping that such a big secret?"

"C'mon Tee, we all know I fell for him hard, and what if he's behind this whole thing."

"We're sisters, Nova. We don't keep secrets from each

other. You know that."

"Tee, I'm going crazy. I don't know what to do anymore."

"Maybe you need to get out of here, go home, spend some time with your family."

"I don't know. How can I just forget about Nia?"

"You've done a pretty good job of doing that the last two weeks or so, haven't you?"

"Wow Tee, you want to come at me like that?"

"That's what sistas do…they tell you like it is, and you, Nova, have been pretty damn selfish lately."

"I know Tee. I know."

"Look, we haven't forgotten Nia, we all here are still looking into a person, and most of us are setting up dates, meetings, whatever you wanna call 'em. You just haven't been around to find out what's going on."

At that precise moment, I knew I had to get away and go home. It was the best thing I could do for myself, for my sisters, and for Nia. I hugged each of them one by one, and told them I would return to the house when I was ready. I apologized to AJ since she took the worst of my selfish behavior. She hugged me so tight, and said "hurry back when you get right."

They walked out of my room, and put my head down for a minute, and knew it was time for me to go back to the place of remembering who I am. I got up, pulled out my duffle bag, and started to pack. I looked over at my dresser, and stared at the picture of me and Nia, smiled, grabbed it and put in with the other things I was taking with me. I picked up my cell phone, and called home. I told my mom, I would be back home by sun down. She sounded so happy to hear me say those words. I had not talked to her in quite a while, and yet her voice made me feel so at ease that I couldn't wait to get home. As I hung up the phone I realized that I had not texted Anenthen back, so opened my messages and replied that maybe we could go out later during the week, but that I was going to home to hang out with my mom that night. Anenthen replied back immediately, and said it was cool. He said he would wait until I was ready to meet him, and he was in no rush. I replied letting him know that I would text later that night or the next day, and I was looking forward to meeting him. He replied with one word: Indeed.

As I walked out of my room, I turned back, and I looked over to Nia's side of the room. I swear I could still see her sitting there on the bed laughing at me and pointing as if I was the crazy one. I smiled at her as I closed the door, walked down the stairs to the common area, and out of the front door. I opened the trunk to my Camaro, and threw my duffle bag in and shut it closed. I loved that car so much, and was so happy when my mom bought it for me. She had no explanation as to how she got the money for it. All she told me was that it was money owed to me, it was my right, my inheritance. When I kept asking about it, she told me leave it at that. I was so happy that I had a brand new car, paid in full, that I didn't question her anymore. I get in my car, put the key in, started it up, and sat there, as I did every time, just to hear that engine roar with such power. It was an awesome feeling. I drove off, and headed home.

As I drove up, and into the driveway, I remember coming home from school as a child, and entering through the side door and into the kitchen. My mom always had a meal on the table when my brother and I got home. She never failed to make sure we would eat. I walked up to the door, she opened it, and there it was, a hot meal sitting on the table. She looked at me, and smiled.

"Welcome home mija."

"Hi Mom."

I hugged her as I walked in, and went over to sit at the table to eat. She followed behind and sat down next to me.

"What's on your mind child."

"Why does something always got to be on my mind?"

"Because I know you, and as far back as I can remember, every since you were you little, whenever you were troubled by something, you always came running."

"Mom, I think I'm going crazy."

"Nonsense. Those dreams bothering you still?"

"How did you know? They're getting worse. I don't know what's real anymore."

She got up from the table. I could tell she was worried about something. She walked over to the stove, and turned on the comal to make some fresh tortillas.

"I was afraid this day would come one day, but you have to get past those dreams. That's all they are…just dreams."

"Mom, they're so real. I've been seeing things I can't explain, and things have been happening to me."

She shook her head and turned to look at me.

"Eat. You need to eat. Look how thin you're getting."

"Yes ma'am."

I sat there for a minute looking at her. I could tell she knew I wasn't eating, so I grabbed my fork and started to eat. After she made a new batch of tortillas, she came over with her plate of food, and sat down to eat with me. I asked her how my brother was doing and she said he was doing great. A smile came over my face knowing that they were doing good because it made me happy. We sat there quiet while we ate, but I could tell she had things on her mind. I couldn't finish eating as I wasn't very hungry. She told me to go lay down, and not to worry as I wouldn't have any dreams tonight. The strangest feeling came over me as I remembered her saying that several times to me while I was growing up, and she was always right about it.

I walked into my old room, and it still looked the same as I left it. It was a small room, but it held so many good memories. I laid down, but couldn't sleep, so I decided to text Anenthen to see what he was doing. He took a while to reply back, but eventually he did. He said he was out with friends, and surprised that I text him. I told him I was too, that is surprised that I texted him, but I thought about his offer to go out, and thought it might be cool to hang out with him. He replied instantly with a "LOL" and "cool, let's do it then." I replied back letting him know that we had a set date.

"Okay, so what would you like to do?" his next text read.

"Let's go to a movie then maybe have a drink," my text replied.

He then asked me to pick out a movie. I told him I would do exactly that and let him know by text tomorrow. After that, the texting stopped, and I was off asleep.

I woke up the next morning, feeling like I slept an entire week, and I didn't have one dream. I woke up with so much energy. I could smell the breakfast my mom was cooking in the kitchen. I was definitely home. I got up, went to wash up, and head to the table before she could yell out for me to get up.

"I thought you were going to sleep all day mija."

"It feels like I did. Guess there's no place like home."

"Here, eat."

"Gracias."

"Oh, you haven't forgotten where you come from Ms. College." I laughed with her.

"No Mom. I haven't forgotten where I come from...I just need to remember who I am."

"Como?"

"Just something I heard lately."

"Such nonsense...you know exactly who you are."

"I wonder sometimes...I wonder."

She stood at the stove just shaking her head.

As I was sitting at the table my phone went off, and she got after me for bringing it into her kitchen. She made me get up and take it out of there and back to my room. Walking through the dining room and the hall, I looked at the text message. It was Anenthen asking what time, what movie theater, and most importantly what movie. I didn't reply right back as I knew she would be calling out for me to hurry back before my food got cold.

She was sitting at the table when I got back. She looked at me like she wanted to say something, but just motioned for me to sit down and eat. I did. Her food was the best, and there was nothing like it. It had its own aroma, and the spices she used brought out her dish's full flavor. I savored every bite like it would be my last. She smiled at me and nodded her head in satisfaction. Once I finished, I took my plate over to the sink to wash it, but she would not let me do so, as it was her kitchen, and she liked things done a certain way. I hugged and thanked her then walked back to my room.

I picked up my phone and replied back to Anenthen letting him know that I was looking up the movie times for later than night. He replied back saying okay and to hit him back when I found out what movie I wanted to see. I put some thought into what we should see. I didn't want to make him see a chick flick with me as he might be bored, nor did I want to see a horror movie as I might jump out my seat and into his, so I went with an action film seeing that there weren't any good comedy showing at the time. I texted him back to let him know the time, place, and movie. He replied back saying he would see me at 6 o'clock for the movie.

As always, I was running late. I decided to call him instead of texting to let him know. He answered. It was the first time I heard his voice. I like it. He had a pleasant voice. He said it was okay that I was running late. Anenthen offered to get the tickets, so when I arrived we could go straight into the movie theater. I agreed that would be the best plan since I would not arrive for another fifteen minutes. We hung up, and I continued to drive over to the movie theater.

My phone rang. For a minute I was nervous that it might be him calling back. I looked at it and realized it was my friend, Duane.

"Yo Slick, what's up Girl?"

"Nada Play'r. Heading out."

"Hey, we going out tonight. You game."

"Gonna have to pass tonight."

"What? You, pass on a night out. I got ya tonight. Don't need nothing, just bring yourself."

"Can't I'm going to the movies."

"With who? Do I know this clown?"

"Stop...he just a dude I met online, and I'm gonna meet him at the movies."

"Slick, you be careful. I don't want you turning out like Nia."

"I hear ya Play'r."

"A'ight, but Imma hit u up in couple of hours…cool."

"Cool…by the way, if we hit it off, I may let him take me out for a drink, so we may see you. I'll talk to you later."

"A'ight, have fun."

As I hung up the phone, I arrived at the movie theater and called him. He answered and told me that he was waiting outside.

"Well, I'm inside," I laughed. "I'll wait at the door for you."

He walked in and I immediately felt like I knew him from somewhere. I was like 'I met him before'. He looked a little different from his picture on his profile. He was six feet tall and average built. I smiled at him and he smiled back.

"Sorry, I didn't mean to be late."

"It's okay because I've already seen the movie."

"What, why didn't you tell me that? We could have picked something else out," "It's not a big deal and you really wanted to see this movie," he said with a laugh.

We walked in to the movie to realize there were not many seats and had to sit in the second row. We really didn't have a chance to say much since the movie had started, so we just sat there and watched it.

As the credits rolled, we got up and walked out of the theater.

"So, you've seen it before?" He laughed and replied,

"Well, this is the third time that I've seen it." I sat there in shock at what he'd said. The expression showed on my face.

"I'm so sorry. I had no idea you had seen it that many times." He smiled as we walked to the parking lot.

"Did you like it?"

"Yes, thank you. I did enjoy the movie. It was not comfortable seeing it up that close though." We continued to talk on our way to our vehicles. It seemed as if neither of us wanted the night to end, so we decided instead of going to have a drink that we would go to his place, and watch another movie and really get to talk to each other.

For a minute, I thought that might have been the wrong idea as I really liked Anenthen, and I didn't want it to end up the same as all the other guys I met online. I still couldn't put my finger on it, but he looked somewhat familiar. The night flew by. We laughed all night and found out we had a lot in common, even with the age difference, as he was a few years older.

Anenthen was a perfect gentleman by keeping his hands to himself and making sure there was plenty of distance between us. I really started feeling comfortable with him, so I moved closer letting him know I was okay with him. Our unique sense of humor came out, and we were joking around with each other. What followed next was the exact thing I was hoping to avoid, but it just felt right.

I woke up the next morning in his arms. It was a good feeling since I wasn't trying to get up, get dressed, or get out as soon as I could. He pulled me closer in toward him.

"Morning, how did you sleep Nova?"

"Hey, I slept good."

"Good."

"I should go though."

"Alright, let me get up."

"Okay."

We got up together, got dressed at the same time, and he walked me to the door and down the stairs to my car. As I was going to get in, he grabbed me, and hugged me.

"I'll call you, okay?"

"Sure."

I said good-bye, got in, drove off, and looked in my rear view mirror as I saw him go back up the stairs to his place. On my way back home, I kept thinking I made a big mistake with him, not because I slept with him, but I slept with him on the first date. Any smart girl knows, it's a huge mistake to sleep with a guy on a first date if he may be potential for something more than a one night stand. And even though that little voice in my head was going off, something in my heart was saying, "no, it wasn't a mistake".

I arrived at home to find my mother in the kitchen. She was sitting at the table.

"Is this how you show respect?"

"Mami, I'm sorry. I should have called you, but I just didn't realize the time."

"I've been up all night, worried that you might have been in an accident, or worse."

"Worse?"

"Come, sit down."

"What's wrong?"

"It's time you know...I can't keep it a secret anymore."

"What Mami...what?"

"Mija, we come from a different background. You're

unique in your own special way. Even more than me or the family."

"Unique, como?"

"We see things, we know things…it goes back generations…way back."

"What are you talking about?"

"Be quiet…listen…Your dreams, they're not dreams. It's called a vision. You can see things…you can see what will happen tomorrow, the day after, next year. You come from a long line of brujahs…some good, some not so good."

"Mami, this is crazy…como witches? You're saying we're witches?"

"Yes mija, but you are unique from the rest of us."

"How?"

"Please understand, and believe me when I tell you this, but it's for your own good that you do not know in what way you are unique. You're special."

"Does this have anything to do with dad?"

"Estas loca…don't talk about him in mi casa. You know I don't like to bring up the past."

"Como no…he was my father. How can I not ask you about him?"

"Listen, I'm telling you this for your own good…When you see something in your visions, know that it is real, and know that you can change the outcome of it, but only if you believe you can."

"Mami, this all sounds surreal, it can't be real, but I trust you and always have…what I don't understand is how every time you say I will not have bad dreams, or rather visions, I don't…how is that possible."

"It's a spell mija…someday, when I pass, you will understand how to use the gift you have."

"Why? Why until you pass...don't talk like that."

"It cannot be passed down to you until I pass...you have the vision, but you don't have the entire gift yet."

She got up from the table, and proceeded to walk out of the kitchen, and into living room to watch t.v.. I didn't know what to say after her last words of our conversation. I just sat there, and taking in everything she said. If what I was seeing weren't dreams, and visions instead, then not only Nia was in serious trouble but so was I. Whatever was in my visions wanted me, and from what I saw, it was not going to stop until it got exactly what it wanted. I had to tell my mom about it, and ask her if she knew what it was in my visions.

I walked into the living room, and she was sitting on the sofa.

"Mom, I have a question."

She didn't respond.

"Did you hear me Mom?"

She sat there like she was in a trance or something. It hit me like a ton of bricks. My mom was the same way I sat when I was seeing my vision when AJ walked into my room. She looked like she was in a different place. It was so weird to see her in that state of mind. However, when I walked up to her to snap her out of it, as AJ did with me, she didn't come out of it. She appeared to truly be out of her body. I was freaked out, and just left the room, with so many unanswered questions.

CHAPTER ELEVEN

I woke up the next morning to the aroma of the food cooking on the stove. I didn't have any of my visions the night before. It was the most sleep I had in such a long a time. I looked over at my phone and noticed I missed a text from Anenthen. With everything I was dealing with, I had forgotten all about our date together, and worrying if he was ever going to contact me again. I got out of bed and walked down the hall and into the kitchen.

"Morning Mom."

"It's about time you get up. Breakfast is ready, and don't tell me your not hungry."

"Actually, I'm starving. Let me wash up."

"Okay, hurry up. I made something special."

"Don't you always. I can never cook like you. The spices… seasonings you use are so unique."

"Just like you. I've been cooking for you like this since you were a kid. It always helps ease your appetite."

I laughed.

"Problem is that I gain so much weight when I'm here."

"Weight? Hush now, you can get back to working it off once you return to campus, Ms. College."

"Mom you're so funny."

I walked out of the kitchen and made my way to the bathroom to wash up and take a shower. The water was so soothing, and felt good splashing against my skin. I closed my eyes, and felt each drop hit against me. *As I opened my eyes, I saw the splash of red against my skin. I looked at it closely. I looked up and there stood George with his throat slashed, and his blood was all over me. I started to scream, but it was if no one heard me, not even my mom. I fell over, and out of the bathtub, and as I got up to turn and open the bathroom door, he was gone and so was the blood.*

I heard a bang on the door.

"Hurry up. You're food is getting cold."

My body was shaking, and I was trying to focus on what was real. I grabbed for my clothes, and put them on even though I was still wet. I rushed out of the bathroom, and into the kitchen. She saw that I was in such distraught state of mind. She came over to me, put her arms around me, and explained that visions could come and go, whenever, wherever. I started to cry.

"Stop that nonsense. It cannot harm you in anyway. Visions come for a reason. It's a warning or way of letting you know what is to come."

"Why me?"

"Because you are mi hija, and thus chosen to continue this gift. There's a purpose, and one day you shall know why you. Now eat."

She expected me to eat after the vision I just had, and even though I was not hungry, I would not dare disrespect her by not eating the food that she put hard work into. The vision of George faded as I took each bite, and it eased my hunger pain.

"Thanks Mom. It was good. I'm going to get on my computer."

"You have homework?"

"It looks like the semester may be done for me. I can always make it up next semester, and play catch up during the summer semester. I'm good."

I walked back to my room, and took out my laptop, and jumped online to see if anyone was on. Some of the girls were online, and I received an instant message from Em. She was telling me about what was going on with everyone. She said that she was still in contact with the guy she was looking into on the site. She updated me on everyone else, and they seemed to be making a little progress of finding out about the men that we did not know in Nia's friend's list.

I was glad that some progress was being made. She asked me about Brackz, and if I had found out anything about his friendship with Nia. I told her not yet, but that I had set up a first meeting with him. She told me to be careful about meeting him, and said maybe I should reconsider. I responded that I really didn't think he was the guy involved in Nia's disappearance. We ended our conversation on that note. It was good to hear from one of my sisters.

I opened another screen and logged into my email account. A message from Brackz was at the top of my inbox. I opened it and read it. He was asking if we could meet in my hometown in two weeks time. He finished his work in New York, and before he flew back to Amsterdam, he wanted to fly to San Antonio and meet me. He proposed we go to dinner, and then do something after, but he would take care of all the plans. I thought about the idea of finally meeting Brackz, but I really wasn't interested in him personally anymore. It was more of wanting to clear him of being involved with Nia's disappearance. Brackz was definitely cool and charming, but he wasn't Anenthen who had pretty much all my attention at this point.

I replied to him and told him to let me know when he was in town, and I would go out to whichever establishment he picked to meet him for dinner. I didn't go into the doing something after, as I was sure I would only be having dinner with him and then end the night. He replied instantly as if he was waiting for me to respond, which gave me a strange feeling. He said he would see me in two weeks and was looking forward to it. I logged off my email account, and jumped on line to the social networking sites.

As I logged on, I saw Maxwell online. He sent me an IM as he saw me online as well. We started a conversation, and before we got past the how are you doing thing, he asked he if could see me. He wanted to hang out and invited me over to his place to watch a movie and have a couple of drinks as friends. I wasn't sure if that was a good idea, but Maxwell and I had so much history, and the last time we went out was good.

Even though I hesitated for a minute, I told him I would be okay with just hanging out if he was okay with it. He agreed to hang out just as friends, and we made plans to meet at his place that weekend. I said my see you soon and talk to you later, and I ended the conversation. I thought to myself that I would finally ask Maxwell about being on Nia's friends' list on all three of the sites she was on. I didn't know what would come from that conversation, but it was time that I confronted him about it.

In talking to Brackz and Maxwell, I found myself wanting to talk to Anenthen all the more, so I decided to call him. It wasn't like me to call anybody, not that I didn't, but I was into texting more than anything else. It was comfortable because emotions or feeling didn't really come into play when you text a person. It was just the easiest way to remain at comfortable distance with someone. Anenthen texted me back after a few minutes. We exchanged texts for about two hours, and then he asked me out again. I was ecstatic that he actually wanted to see me again. I was so sure that he thought I wasn't worth his time after our first date. I thought, in the back of my head, sleeping with him on the first date would be a deal breaker of really being able to get to know him. But, I was finding out that Anenthen was truthful in his message to me about him being unique and unlike any other dude. I hadn't met anyone like him before and it was so refreshing. We planned to meet that night at a bar I had never been to, so I was looking forward to going there and seeing him again.

The night seemed to take forever to come around. Meeting Anenthen that night might have played a factor in the time dragging by so slowly. As I was getting ready to leave, my phone rang. By the ring tone playing, I knew it was Maxwell. I hit the ignore button and let it go to the voice mail. I told my mom that I was leaving for the night, and would be home late, but that I would be home. I think that eased her mind. She told me good night, and I walked out the side door and over to my car. It took me twenty minutes to get to the place. I had passed by it several times, but never took it for a hangout that I would find myself at with friends.

I walked up the stairs and the bouncer opened the door. I walked in. The place was small. It had the bar against the wall as you walked in, and several high tables and bar stools in the middle of the place. There were a couple of pool tables next to the jukebox, and an area with several sofas and coffee tables on the left. The place was lit up by red lights, so it was hard to get a clear view of anyone's face from a distance. I walked up to the bar and ordered a bud light. The female bartender told me it was two dollars. I tried to pull out my money, but before I could, a voice told her to put it on his card. I looked back and it was Anenthen.

"I'm sitting over there. Grab your beer. C'mon."

"Okay, hold on. Let me get it."

We proceeded to walk over to the area of the sofas and sat down.

"I see you found the place."

"Yep, I did. Good directions, thanks."

"No problem."

"So what you been up to?"

"Just hanging out at my mom's place. Catching up with her."

"Cool."

"And you?"

"Same shit, different day."

We both laughed. Anethen had a very nice smile that showed off his dimples. He was very attractive, smart, and funny. He had all the qualities I look for in a guy, and more. We sat there for the next hour just shooting the breeze, and talking about different things. Then asked if I played pool. I told him I did, but was a bit rusty since I hadn't played in a while.

"Let's go play."

"Alright."

We walked over to one of the pool tables, placed our beers on the nearest table, and he began to rack.

"Ladies first."

"You sure you want me to go first?"

"I racked, didn't I."

"Yep. Okay."

After a couple of games, laughing and talking, he realized that I knew how to play the game, in fact, he learned that I was quite good at it.

"I think I've been hustled."

"Hustled? By who? Me, hustle you? I would never. It's luck."

"Luck, my ass."

"You know how to play."

"Just a bit."

"Right. So, where did you learn?'

"That's one thing I do remember my dad teaching me as kid."

"Your dad, huh?"

"Yea, I don't remember a lot about him, but I do remember him showing how the game is played."

"What's your dad's name?"

"Armand."

"And your mom's name?'

"Celia."

"Do they live here in San Antonio?"

"My mom does…my dad passed away when I was a teen-ager."

"Sorry to hear that Nova."

"No biggie, I hadn't seen him since I was a kid."

"Why?"

"He moved away when my brother and I were very young. He never came back. Mom raised us herself to the best of her ability."

"Where did your dad move to?"

"Houston, is what mom told us."

"Was his last name Salinas too?"

"Nope. I have my mom's last name. Never figured that one out, but I guess it was for the best."

"I see…so, he never contacted you again."

"I remember him trying to contact us. I think he wanted me to go up to Houston for a visit, some type of family gathering, but mom refused, and that was the last I remember of him trying to see us."

"Did your mom ever tell you why she wouldn't let you go to Houston?"

"You know you ask a lot of questions…but, she just told me we didn't have the money to send me on a flight down there."

"I'm sorry. I didn't mean to pry, but it's an interesting story you got there."

"I guess, if you say so."

I found it strange that Anenthen was so interested in my family background. I figured he was really trying to get to know the person standing in front of him. You really can't know a person via computer or phone, and it's not until you actually come face to face with a person that you begin to get a sense of who they really are. People can pretend to be anybody on a screen, but in person, it's hard to be somebody you're not, especially if the other person has a keen sense of knowing when somebody is lying or telling the truth. And that came very naturally to me, as it seemed it was one of Anenthen's natural qualities as well. By the time last call was made, we had played our fair share of pool with me winning most of the games. We decided to call it a night. I told him I had to go to the bathroom, but would be quick about it.

"Take your time. I'm in no hurry."

"Okay then."

As I came out of the ladies room, and walked backed over toward him, I realized that I was nervous about his expectations for the rest of the night.

"You look like something is on your mind. Don't worry, I have no expectations of having sex with you tonight Nova."

"Who said I was worried. Hate to burst your bubble, but

you're the only one thinking of sex. Who said I wanted to have sex with you tonight or for that fact ever again."

"Whatever Nova. You act like you didn't like it."

"And you act like I can't wait to trip and fall…on top of you that is."

We both starting laughing. He pulled me in to hug me, and then we walked out of the place, and each made our way to our own cars. I got in and drove home.

The weekend came around before I knew the week had passed. Anenthen and I continued to talked via text everyday for several hours. He kept inquiring about my childhood and my family. So, I decided to reciprocate the gesture. I had forgotten about the plans I set with Maxwell until he called me and reminded me that he had everything set up for our movie hang out at his place. I rushed to get ready by throwing on a pair of jeans, t-shirt, and sneakers. It wasn't like it was a date, but rather two friends just hanging out.

I arrived at his place and the memories of hanging out there my freshman year came back to me. The place had not changed a bit, and its exterior in all its beauty still amazed me as if it was the first time I was seeing again. I was getting out of my car as he walked over and opened my door for me.

"Hey."

"You look nice tonight."

I laughed and shook my head.

"You got to be kidding, right?"

"You always look nice regardless what you're in."

"Thanks Maxwell."

"Well, are you hungry because I can have something delivered before we start the movie."

"Actually, I'm not really hungry. How 'bout we just chill and watch the movie."

"Alright. Come inside."

I walked into the same house I thought I'd never enter again. I loved his house, but it felt so empty this time as if something was missing.

"Let's go into the theater."

"Okay, lead the way. I don't wanna get lost."

"You lost? I don't think that will truly ever happen to you Ms. Salinas. You might go off the path for a minute, but you will never be lost."

"Uh, alright. What movie will we be seeing?"

"Something I know you haven't seen. Just wait."

We walked into the media room and sat down. The preview starts to roll as he grabbed my hand. I looked at him as to suggest 'What are you doing?'

"Do you want a glass of wine or a drink?"

"Uh, I don't know."

"C'mon, I'm not gonna take advantage of you…we're friends remember."

"Okay then. A glass of Moscato would be nice."

"I'll be right back."

It was an awkward moment for a just a minute. The room was silent even though the previews were playing. The intro to the movie began and he still was not back. I sat back and smiled at the screen. It was the same movie that Anenthen and I went to watch. I felt like it was some kind of sign. Maxwell walked back in with two glasses and popcorn.

"Here you go."

"Shhh! I'm watching the movie."

He smiled at me then sat down and handed me a glass and placed the popcorn between us. As the credits rolled, he asked me if I liked it.

"I already seen it, but yes, it's an awesome movie."

He looked at me with a strange expression, but then proceeded to smile.

"How about dinner?"

"The popcorn was enough."

"Another glass of wine?"

"I'm good. But maybe we can just talk for a little while. I wanted to ask you something."

"Sure, let's go to the living area, and I'll put some music on."

We walked out of the media room, down the hall, and sat in the living area. He walked over to grab the remote on the mantel over the fireplace, and put some music on. He sat down next to me and we started talking about irrelevant things that lead into reminiscing about our time together. I was trying to get to the point of why I was there and wanted to ask about his and Nia's friendship. Before I could say anything, he leaned in close to me as if he was going to kiss me. I back my head away from him.

"What was that?"

"What?"

"Why did you move away?

"Because you tried to kiss me."

"Yeah, and?"

"We're not going there. We're friends now and that's all we are gonna be."

"Nova get your mind right. We're never gonna be just friends. We are always going to be tied together. You can't deny that fact."

"What are you talking about? How can I be tied to someone who has no respect for me...someone who threw away everything we had for something he obviously got then got rid of and now wants this back."

"You still have no clue do you?"

"Clue? The only clue I have is that you keep lying to me, and now you have me over in a pretense that this is just a hang out amongst friends."

"Who is he Nova?"

"Who is who?"

"The dude your obviously seeing and falling for."

"I'm not here for that Maxwell."

"Then why are you here if not to be with me?"

"I want to know what was going on between you and Nia. I know you are on her friends' list on all three of the sites she was on. What I don't understand is why, especially since you two claimed to hate each other."

"Nova, don't ask questions you really don't want the answer to."

"What the hell do you mean? You know what...I'm done here. Don't call me, don't text, don't look for me...I'm done."

"You don't know what you're saying, so I will let you leave for now, but you will be back."

"Wateva Maxwell....so damn full of yourself."

I looked at him, turned and walked out of the house. I drove for miles that night thinking about him saying for me not to ask questions I really didn't want the answer to. I drove Loop 1604, which took me all around the city. As I was going to make a second trip around the loop, I decided to call Anenthen.

"Hey you."

"What's up Nova?"

"What are you up to?"

"Nothing really. Just chilling at home. Thinking about going out."

"Want some company?"

"You sure you want to be around me…you may not be able to resist this time."

I laughed.

"I'm sure I'd like to hang out with you tonight."

"Alright, c'mon over. I'll be waiting for you."

I got off the loop and headed for IH-10 and over to his place. I was still mad at Maxwell, but understood that it was partially my fault as well. I knew I shouldn't have went over to his place. I arrived at Anenthen's and called him so he could open the gate. I parked and went up the stairs. He opened the door and smiled at me. That smile took everything away that I was feeling. It scared me so much that seeing him could make me feel that happy. I walked in and he closed the door behind me.

"Make yourself at home. You wanna a beer?"

"Sure."

I walked over to the couch and sat down. He walked up to me, handed me the beer, and made a comment if he was going to be okay sitting next to me.

"What do you mean?"

"Well, I'm not sure, if you gonna jump on me or something. I mean you haven't seen me in a couple of days. And I am irresistible."

I starting laughing,

"You're crazy!"

"I know…so what's up?"

"Nada…that's Spanish for "nothing"."

"I see…okay."

"Do you know any Spanish?"

"No, not like I need to though."

"You're in San Antonio…of course you need to….guess Imma have to teach you."

"Is that right?"

"Yes sir."

We sat back and just starting talking. It seemed so easy to talk to him. We had things in common and then we had things we didn't, but that's what kept the conversation going. He put on a movie, and we continued to drink and talk. He placed his hand upon me and started to rub down my thigh. It felt so good to have him touch me again. I placed my hand on his hand. His hand slip up toward my face and he pulled my chin toward him and kissed me so softly. I smiled at him and kissed him again. He grabbed my waist and pulled me over and on top of him.

We started kissing, and his hands were sliding up and down my back, as my hands were sliding up and down his chest. His hand slid up toward the back of neck, and he grabbed my hair and pulled my head back away from him. I felt his lips upon my neck. I reached for his neck in a chocking position and kissed him. It started to get very hot as we kept at it. I felt the sensation of blacking out coming upon me and I realized that the feeling wasn't of me blacking out, but rather of me having some type of out of body experience during the point of pure ecstasy. As I was at that point, he said something that stopped everything in a split second.

"Damn Mama."

I opened my eyes, looked at him.

"What did you say?"

"I said, damn mama."

I got off him, and he looked at me with a strange look.

"Did I say something wrong?"

"Uh no. It just caught me off guard."

"You okay?"

"Yeah, actually I'm great."

We looked at each other and laughed. He stood up, grabbed my hand, and led me into his room. That night we had sex, and it was better than first time, as I realized who he reminded me of. The minute he called me mama, the vision of my dream guy came flashing before me and so did all the conversations that I had with him. I fell asleep that night in his arms.

E. A. Lopez

CHAPTER TWELVE

I tipped toe into the house, like if I already didn't know she knew I hadn't been home that night. I even tried to throw her off guard and enter the house through the front door. As I walked in she was sitting in the living room.

"Why you sneaking in like you're sixteen years old and have a curfew?"

"Aye Mom…you scared me."

"So you gonna tell me who this guy is since he has kept you from coming home on two occassions?"

"His name is Anenthen Morrison."

"What type of man keeps you out all night?"

"He's a good guy Mom, and I'm a big girl. He's not forcing me to do anything I don't want to do."

"I would hope not."

"Mom, I need to talk to you about my visions…I need your help in understanding what they all mean."

"I can't help you understand your vision mija. Only you know what they mean."

"Then look at your visions and tell me what is going to happen in my future because I can't see me there."

"Let me explain…we can't see what is going to happen amongst our own. It's the one curse that comes with this gift."

"How that can be?"

"It can't be explained…just trust your instincts as they will never do you wrong. Always remember that."

She walked out of the living and into her room. It was the first time I came home and she was cooking a meal for me. I started to wonder if she was okay. I walked passed her room and into mine. My duffle bag was packed and sitting on the bed. I turned to look toward her room. She was standing at my door.

"It's time for you to get on with your life. You can't hide here forever, even though I would love you to. You have to get back to campus and finish college. You have to get back to who you are."

"Mom, you gonna be alright?"

"Of course, we Salinas women come from a strong line of blood...tough skin too."

I walked over to her.

"No tears...no good-byes...just smiles."

I looked at her and knew that one day I could only hope to be as strong as she was. I picked up my duffle bag, walked out the door, got in my car, and headed to the sorority house.

The music was blasting as I drove. I could see the girls looking out the window, and AJ came running out.

"We missed you!"

"Hey Girl"

I smiled and looked up to see the window of my room. I saw Nia standing there looking down at me with a smile on her face, and even though it was only a vision, it brought such joy to me.

"Nova...glad to see your back. We were 'bout to send out the search party for you."

"Thanks Tee. It's so good to be home...home away from home."

"Well, they're all waiting for you inside."

"How you know I was gonna be back today."

"Strangest thing, we just had a feeling...guess it's that sista love."

Tee and I walked in. AJ had made her way back into the house before we did. Everybody was standing around, and then they rushed me. We were hugging, and joking around with each other.

"Where's Luna?"

"She took off Nova. She said told us she had some things to do."

"Oh ok...cool. It's no big deal."

"Yeah, it is...Right Jules?"

"AJ, it's cool."

"Welcome back Nova...your room has been so empty."

"Thanks Jules. Well, not to cut this home coming short 'cuz it is about me...but, I want to unpack, and then we can catch up tonight."

"That's cool...go on. We can talk later."

I walked up the stairs and made my way down the hall and into mine and Nia's room. The girls didn't touch a thing. It was exactly as I left it. I took the picture of Nia and me and placed it back on my dresser. I started to unpack my things, but was overwhelmed by so many memories that I shared in that room. I feared that seeing Nia smiling at me from the window wasn't part of a vision but rather a hopeful thought. I feared too much time had passed and Nia would never be found at this point. It was a known fact that people who went missing for too long were either never found or found dead. I hated to think that could be a possibility, but I had to come to some realization for my own peace of mind.

I looked out the window and stared at the campus. I had to go talk to my advisor first thing Monday morning to see if I could salvage the semester. I had missed so many classes, and the semester was at midterm. My door opened, and I turned to see who was there.

"I heard you were back."

"What's up Luna?"

"Why'd you bother?"

"Bothered? With what?"

"Coming back...we're at mid term."

"Yeah, I know, but my place is here. You have a problem with that?"

"I have a problem with you abandoning your sister...and the sorority."

"You think I wanted to...there's so much you don't know. I've had to deal with some things...now that I have, I'm back." She laughed at me. Shook her head.

"No Nova, there's so much you don't know. As far as I'm concerned you might as well stay gone."

"It's like that?"

"Yeah, it's like that."

"So be it...you know where the door is at." She rolled her eyes at me, and walked out the door.

I heard Tee coming up the stairs as she was calling out my name. She knocked and came in the room. She told me everybody was going to eat, and wanted to know if I was joining. I almost told her no but realized I needed to spend some time with them and get back to being part of a sisterhood. We all gathered up in common area and decided to order pizza instead and just shoot the breeze to catch up. I hadn't laughed so hard with them in a while. Then, we got serious about things as they brought up Nia's name.

You could feel the tension build up between Luna and my-self. I told everybody that I asked Maxwell about his relationship with Nia. I also told them about Brackz and Anenthen. Every time I mentioned Anenthen's name, a smile would appear. The girls noticed that I seemed happy when I talked about him. As Luna got up to confront me, her phone rang.

"Hello…."

A silence came over as if she was listening intensely and motioning for us to shut up.

"Are you sure? I'll be right over."

She hung up the phone, turned and looked at us. She didn't say anything at first, then starting tearing up.

"What is it? Is it Nia?"

"That was Nia's mom. S.A.P.D called her. Someone fitting the description of Nia was seen in New York. Nia's mom asked me to fly there with her to talk to N.Y.P.D."

A sigh of relief came over me before I realized that it had to be a huge coincidence that Brackz was in New York, and now Nia was sighted there. The girls were all trying to get their thoughts together as they were questioning Luna for more information. I quietly walked away without being noticed and made my way up to the computer in my room. I logged on to my email account to check if Brackz had emailed me. He hadn't. So, I clicked on new messages and composed an email asking him for the details of when and where we were going to meet. I also asked if he was still in New York. I sent it off. I wasn't sure how long it was going to take for him to reply, but I stayed on for a few minutes. It was a long shot that he was on, but sure enough he replied. It always seemed like he knew when I was going to email him. I opened it

E. A. Lopez

and read the message. He told me he had left New York already and was in route to Texas, but had a couple stops on the way. His plane into San Antonio would arrive on Friday night, and he was going to be staying at the JW Marriott. He continued to tell me that he had everything planned for Saturday night and couldn't wait to meet me.

I responded to his email and asked when he left New York. I also asked where he wanted me to meet him since he was not giving much information about our dinner plans. An email arrived back immediately. He told me he left New York a couple days back and headed out to visit friends in another state. He asked if we could meet at his hotel in the lobby around five thirty in the afternoon. I thought to myself that he wasn't saying a whole lot about anything. It was kind of mysterious, but I agreed to meet him at the hotel on Saturday in my response back to him. His emails stopped.

I could hear the girls anxiously pacing downstairs, as I assumed that Luna had already left to meet Mrs. Carmichael at the San Antonio International Airport. I picked up my cell phone and sent Anenthen a text message. He replied immediately. That feeling I felt every time I was around him came over me, and I could feel myself smiling even though he wasn't around. We talked via text for a couple of hours and decided to meet up at the same spot as before. I got dressed and went downstairs.

"Where do you think you're going?"

"Hey Tee, I didn't see you standing there."

"Yep, I noticed."

"Gonna head out and meet Anenthen."

"So, do we ever get meet this guy?"

"If it goes somewhere, yeah definitely."

"Alright Girl…enjoy your night. See you when you get

back, if you get back tonight."

"That depends, I guess."

I walked out the door and headed toward my car. I drove
over to the place we first met up at. The female bartender was behind the bar serving up drinks.

"Hey Girl, I remember you from the other night. What's
your poison tonight?"

"Same thing…I'll take a bud light."

"Alright, I got you."

I handed her my card and told her to keep an open tab.
I went over to sit in the sofa area. I placed my beer on the table
in front of me and looked at the time. He was running late, but I
was cool with that since I felt comfortable in the place. The door
opened, and I looked over to see if it was him. It wasn't. It opened
several more times before he made his way through the door. He
smiled and walked over.

"Sorry, I didn't realize there would be traffic on my way
over."

"It's okay…I'll only have to deduct a point."

"O' you keeping score."

I smile at him.

"Aren't you?"

He laughed.

"You damn right I am now."

The bartender walked over since there weren't may people
in the place and asked if he would like something to drink. He
requested a bud light, and I asked her to put that on my tab.

"O' I see ya doing it up big like that."

"Yep, big spending…a whole two dollars."

He sat down next to me and the conversation started. It was

always a different topic. We could talk for hours with a few pauses but then the conversation would start back up. I asked him if he wanted to shoot pool again. He looked at me, shook his head, and told me he would never get hustled by me again. I couldn't help but to just crack up. He told me he had to go to the restroom and excused himself. As I sat there taking in the music, the bartender came back over and asked if we wanted another round. I told her to go ahead bring another one. I heard the door open, so I turned to my right to see who was entering the place. I couldn't believe it. Of all the places in San Antonio, he had to walk into to that one that night. He walked over as Anenthen was walking back to sit down.

"What's up Ms. Salinas?"

I looked up at him.

"Just chilling…you know."

"Hey, what's up man?"

"What's up?"

"Anenthen, this is Maxwell."

"So, I see you slumming tonight Nova."

Anenthen stood up as I reached for his hand and motioned for him to ignore it.

"Naw, as I see it, I took a step up."

Maxwell laughed.

"Yea, if you say so."

"You got a problem dude?"

"Naw, but you are if you don't stay outta of this."

I looked at Maxwell and got up. Anenthen then stood up and pulled me back. He walked over to Maxwell. He was looking down on him. I didn't hear what he said to him, but Maxwell walked off, and he came back to sit down.

"You alright mama?"

"Yea, I'm good. What did you say to him?"

"I just asked him to take a walk and leave you alone."

I looked over at Maxwell. He was standing at the bar, and I could see him looking at me through the mirror. But he wasn't mad, it appeared he had some fear in him. I had never seen him like that before. I looked at Anenthen in disbelief and didn't say anything else about it.

"Let's get outta here."

"Alright."

We got up and walked out the bar.

"Oh damn, I forgot my card. I'll be right back. Okay?"

I walked back inside and asked the bartender to close out my tab.

"Nova, don't go with him."

"Stop Maxwell."

"I'm serious this is not about me…it's about you. He's not what he appears to be."

"You're drunk…just leave me alone."

As I started to walk away, he grabbed my arm, and I noticed the fear on his face. I looked at him, and he turned toward the door. Anenthen had walked back in to see what was taking me so long. I looked over at the door and felt Maxwell's hand let go of me. I turned to look at Maxwell and then walked away. Anenthen opened the door for me and walked me over to my car.

"You coming over tonight."

I didn't answer for a minute as I was in thought about Maxwell's reaction to Anenthen.

"Yeah…I'll follow you."

"Alright, be careful."

I drove behind Anenthen but my mind wasn't paying attention to where I was going. We arrived at his place, and went upstairs. I sat down on his couch. He looked down at me and could tell I had something on my mind.

"Let's just go lay down tonight."

"That's a good idea."

We laid down and he placed his arm around me. I felt so safe and soon was sound asleep.

"Who is this?"

She giggled. I opened my eyes and there stood Nia.

"You have the strangest timing."

"And you my sister have no idea who you are sleeping with."

"What the hell you talking about. You don't even know him."

"I know something you don't. I know something you don't."

"Nia, stop acting like a child."

She stood there and from behind her, I saw that hand, the same wicked hand I've seen time and time again, grab her throat. She laughed as it slashed her throat and she dropped to the ground. I screamed and Anenthen jumped up.

"Are you okay? What happened?"

I put my head into his chest as he wrapped his arms around me.

"It was just a bad dream."

"You were screaming like someone was killing you."

"Not me, my friend."

"The friend you told me is missing?"

"Yes…she was killed."

"Nova, look at me. It was just a dream. It will be okay."

He pulled me in closer toward him. I felt a little safer, but I couldn't go back to sleep. I stayed up the rest of the night and watched him sleep peacefully.

He woke the next morning and got up.

"I gotta get to work mama."

"I gotta get home."

"You can stay here a bit longer just lock up after you leave."

"No, I really gotta get going. I'm exhausted."

"You didn't go back to sleep?"

"I couldn't."

"Damn."

"It's not your fault."

"Maybe we should have just had sex."

I laughed at him.

"Crazy!"

"You know it."

"Walk me out?"

"You got it."

He walked me downstairs and out to my car. I hugged him, and he kissed me on my forehead. I looked up at him because that was the first time he ever did that. He smiled at me. I smiled back then got into my car and drove off.

I watched him through the rear view mirror. It reminded me of the first time I was there. So much had changed since then. I thought about Maxwell, and then I thought about Nia. I opened my phone and texted Maxwell, but he didn't reply. I decided to see if he would pick up the phone, but he didn't. I got back to the house and everyone was gone to class. I went upstairs and laid down. I closed my eyes and hoped that I'd fall asleep without any more visions.

CHAPTER THIRTEEN

Friday had finally approached, and I wasn't looking forward to my dinner date with Brackz on Saturday, but I was interested in finding out how he knew Nia. Anenthen and I had made plans for the night. I asked him if we could go to a new place or maybe hang out in one of the clubs downtown. His suggestion caught me off guard, as it was the same place I met Maxwell and George.

I thought about George in a passing minute. I still didn't understand how his murder went unsolved. I was the only person that knew of that night, and I knew I should have went to the police, but I was so afraid that I could be the person that caused his death. I could hear all my sisters walking out the door for class. I couldn't wait to talk to my advisor to see if I could re-enroll in my courses or if I just had to withdraw from them. I was hoping that I would be allowed back into some of my classes, so I wouldn't have to repeat them the following semester.

I knew Brackz was coming into town. I got up and went over to the computer to check any messages I had. I pretty much had given up on the social network sites, as I was keeping myself busy with Anenthen. I logged on to my email account and sure enough there was a message from Brackz with the subject line "Almost there". I opened and read his message. His same old charming self came out through his words. He seemed excited that he was going to finally meet me. I knew he might be disappointed if he realized my true intention in meeting him. I replied back and told him I would see him soon. I logged off before any other of his messages could come through.

I decided to head over to the gym and get a workout in before my date with Anenthen. I hadn't been to the gym in a while, and I was feeling it. I entered the building. Jules and Em were already on the treadmills. They waved for me to come over. I jumped onto the open treadmill next to them.

"Hey, did anyone hear back from Luna yet?"

"Naw Girl, you know Luna…she's keeping us in suspense for as long as possible."

"I don't know what's up with her these day. She been acting weird ever since you took off Nova."

"Really?"

"Yeah, it's been crazy around here. We all walking on egg shells when she around."

"Why?"

"Just to avoid a confrontation with her."

"Well, she came at me and we had some words. I know it's not the last of it."

We continued to chat and workout. It was good to be back and hanging with them two. They were still tight as the first day I met them. There were rumors that they were too tight, but we all knew that was bullshit. After thirty minutes on the machine, I decide to head over and work out my legs, so I told them I would see them back at the house. They asked if I wanted to hang out with them that night, but I had to decline.

"Sorry sistas, but I got a hot date with a very good looking guy."

"So we hear he's made quite an impression on you."

"Damn, who's been talking."

I left and headed over to do some leg extensions. I planned on doing several sets, but I looked up and noticed Maxwell walked into the gym. I walked over to the area where he was working out.

"Hey."

"What's up Ms. Salinas?"

"Nada…what's up with you? I called you a couple of times."

"Yeah, I know. I've just been busy."

"Everything alright Maxwell. You haven't been acting yourself lately."

"Look Nova, you know where I stand and what I want. Your boy, the one you was with the other night. He's bad news."

"What do you mean?"

"Nova, he means you more harm than good. Please believe me."

"Damn you Maxwell. I'm not falling for this shit again."

"I'm being straight this time. If you don't believe me…ask him about his past."

"You're crazy…but, I will because he, unlike you Maxwell has never lied to me. That's something I come to count on from him."

"Then ask."

He walked away from me, but looked back. He didn't smile, but rather just gave me a cold stare. I just stared back at him as he walked away. I headed over to the showers, cleaned up, and then walked back to the house.

The night arrived before I was ready to meet Anenthen. I called him and told I would be a little late and apologized. Remembering that he was late the last time, he told me it wasn't a problem and would wait for me at the bar. I rushed to my car and to get downtown as fast as possible. I didn't want to keep him waiting. I approached a parking lot, but it was full, so I tried several others, but they were all full. The only place that had parking was the garage, so I had no choice but to park there. I drove up, gave the attendant the parking fee.

"There's parking on the 5th floor…have a good night."

That's was the last place I wanted park. I got to the 5th and looked around. I didn't see anyone in sight. I parked, got out of my car, and started to walk toward the elevator. The lights started to flicker, and I turned corner to reach for the button. The lights went off completely. I turned to check if anyone was behind me. I couldn't see anything. I heard the elevator bell ring as the door opened. I turned to walk in and there stood George. I froze and backed away hoping the doors would close, but he stepped out and walked toward me. I closed my eyes hoping that he would be gone when I opened them. I felt a hand grab my shoulder and I screamed.

"Are you okay Ma'am?"

It was a guard on duty.

"Yes sir…I was just frightened because the lights went off."

"We've been having that problem for several weeks now. I'll get the elevator for you."

The elevator came back up, and I stepped in and thanked him for his help. I arrived at the bottom floor, and made my way to the club. I walked in and looked around for Anenthen. He was standing at the bar as he said he would be. He was dressed casual but made it look good. He turned as if he could tell I walked in the door. I smiled and waved at him.

"Same thing tonight? Or you gonna change your drink up?"

"I think I'll take a vodka tonight."

"You got it."

He waved down the bartender and ordered my drink. I looked around to make sure I didn't see Maxwell anywhere in sight as the place was his usual hangout.

"So, you been here before?"

"I can't lie...I've been here on numerous occasions."

"Do tell Nova."

"I rather not. The place hasn't changed though...it still has the same atmosphere going on."

"I heard this was an unusual club."

"What do you mean?"

"Well, it said that the place is filled with people from an online social site and unless you're on that site you can't get in."

"So how do I get in cuz I don't know what site your talking about."

"It's called Profyle.com, and I believe you are very well known on that site."

"True, I do have a profile on that site but well known... don't flatter me."

"I'm just letting you know what I've heard."

"Then how did you get in? Because I've never seen you on that site."

"You've never seen the user name Anenthen on that site, but I am on it. You haven't been online for awhile. Care to explain?"

"No!"

"It's okay...I think I have a feeling why you haven't been on."

"Now, don't flatter yourself."

I grabbed my drink and walked away from him. He grabbed my arm. I turned to look back at him and smiled.

"Going somewhere?"

"Just taking a walk around the place."

I notice someone staring at me through the mirror behind the bar. I couldn't get a good view of him, but I swore he looked like Brackz or at least look like the picture I saw of Brackz online. He turned to walk toward the crowd and made his way to the back.

"I gotta use the ladies room...I'll be right back...can you hold this?"

Anenthen looked toward the back of the club.

"Okay, I'll wait for you here at the bar."

I hurried to catch up to the person that looked like Brackz. I was pushing people out of my way, but he disappeared into the crowd. I kept walking and finally made my way to the very back where the restrooms were located. I decided to go to use the ladies room as not to lie to Anenthen when I saw a view of Maxwell's backside hanging out in the V.I.P. section. I walked over there and grabbed his arm to turn him around. I planned on letting him know I was there and I didn't want him starting trouble with Anenthen.

He turned around, but it wasn't Maxwell. It was some guy who looked very similar to him.

"Oh, I'm sorry. I thought you were someone I knew."

"That's okay sweetie. Nova, right?"

"Yeah, do I know you?"

"Nope, but I seen your profile. Nice."

"Uh, thanks...I guess. Excuse me."

I pushed my way through the crowd again and made my way back to Anenthen.

"Hey, it's kinda crazy in here tonight, do you mind if we

check out early."

"Exactly what I was thinking. You okay mama? Looks like you seen a ghost or something."

"I'm fine. Can we just leave."

"Sure let me close out my tab."

Anenthen closed his tab, and we left.

"Where did you park?"

"At the garage? You?"

"Across the street. How about I give you a ride over to your car and you follow me home?"

"Perfect."

We crossed the street, and I was so relieved that he offered to drive me to the garage and directly to my car. We got to the garage and drove up to the fifth floor. The lights were on and he stopped right behind my Camaro.

"You gonna be okay to drive."

"I'm good. I only had that one drink."

"Alright, I'll wait and follow you outta here."

He did just that and proceeded to follow me back to his place. We arrived and he opened the gate. I drove in and we parked. We walked up stairs and into his place. I sat on his couch, and he walked into to the kitchen to get us a couple of beers. He turned on the t.v. and sat next to me. He pulled me toward him as I laid my head on his chest. I could feel his heart beat.

He put his hand on my chin and pulled my face up to look at him. We both smiled at each other. He reached down to kiss me. It was the same soft kiss he always gave. I didn't feel lightning strike when he kissed me as I did with Maxwell. His kiss was different, it was special as it made fell safe. I hadn't felt anything like it before I couldn't explain the safety behind it but it was part of the reason I fell for him. Neither of us said anything more in that moment. We sat and watched a movie for a little while and then he grabbed my hand and off we went to his bedroom.

We started to undress each other while we kissed and touched. My hand looked so light against his body as he was much darker than me, but I loved how our complexion complimented one another. His body felt so warm next to mine. I don't know if I was shivering because I was somewhat totally naked or if I was shaking because I was nervous as this felt like none of the times before. He laid me down on his bed and continued to caress my body. His lips pressed against mine and then moved down toward my neck. It was a very sensitive area for me, and he well knew that. My back arched, and I couldn't help but to let him know it felt good. I ran my hand down his back. My nails dug into his flesh a little, but he gave his approval. It was a night of pure pleasure as we reached a climax at the same time.

"You okay mama."

"I am so okay. You're so awesome."

He laughed.

"Glad it's meet your approval."

"You know it."

"You weren't too bad yourself."

I laughed.

"I think I'm in love with you Anenthen."

"I think you're in lust with me Nova especially after I put in that work."

The room got silent. I didn't know how to take that response, but I was so exhausted that I feel asleep in his arms.

We woke the next morning still in each others' arms. I told him I should go. He asked if I wanted breakfast.

"I'm not really hungry, but thanks. I do appreciate the offer."

He walked me to the door and down to the stairs that lead to the parking lot. We said our good-bye there. It was the first time he didn't walk me all the way to my car. I felt like I shouldn't have let my guard down and opened myself up like that. I wanted to kick myself for saying what I said. I knew I fell hard for him, but I didn't know if he was ready to hear those words.

I replayed everything in my head that happened that night, every word said, every kiss, every touch felt, every moment that made time stand still. I arrived back at the house, and walked in the common area. Rae-Rae was sitting there watching t.v.

"He something special, huh?"

"Yeah Rae-rae, he is."

"Then don't let that go…it only comes around once…maybe twice if you're lucky."

"I hear ya. Well, Imma rest up for dinner tonight. I have a dinner with Brackz, and I'm hoping to put an end to him being part of Nia's disappearance, so I can get on with my own socializing for my own reasons."

"Just be careful tonight, okay?"

"I will. I'll let y'all know where I'm at as soon as I find out where we are going."

I walked up the stairs and into my room. I laid on the bed and continued to think on things. My mind was racing and for once it had nothing to do with visions. I couldn't rest. My phone rang. By the ring tone, I knew it was Anenthen.

"Hey you."

"What's up mama?"

"Just chilling for the moment."

"Cool…I need to talk to you."

"Okay, what's on your mind."

"I'm leaving town Nova. My job called me this morning after you left and I'm getting assigned to another office out of state."

"When will you be back?"

"Unfortunately, I won't. It's a long term move, and I've been waiting and wanting the opportunity to promote into this position. It's available now, and I can't turn it down."

"Can I ask if your decision was based on what I told you last night."

"No mama. My decision would have been the same regardless if you have not told me your feelings for me."

"You gotta do what you gotta do. I understand."

"Are you okay?"

"Of course, I'm okay. People come and people go…they change with the seasons. Good luck."

"Thanks. We'll keep in touch."

"Yeah, of course. I gotta go. You be safe out there."

"Bye mama."

I hung up the phone as those last two words stuck my head. My heart dropped and I felt a pain like no other I have ever felt before and yet, my body felt so numb. I laid in my bed motionless. Tears ran down my eyes. I looked up to the ceiling and cried out.

"Why would you do this to me? Why would you allow him in to enter my life? Why…when you knew I would only be hurt in the end?" With those words said, my body went into total exhaustion. I blacked out.

I slept the entire morning into the afternoon and cried every minute in my sleep. I didn't have any dreams. I didn't have any visions. All I kept hearing was him say, "Bye mama". I woke up with tears still in my eyes. I remember my dream guy and him telling me in one of my visions that he had to go and I wouldn't see him anymore. I realized it was my vision letting me know what the future was going to hold, but I just didn't know at the time.

All I wanted to do was call him and ask him not leave, but it wouldn't be fair for me to do such a thing. How could I ask him to give up something he wanted to do before he even knew me? It was a selfish thought and, for one second, I almost acted on it. I got up, walked over to the window, and just stared into sky. I wasn't looking for anything in particular, but I was hoping for an answer that never came. I walked over to my computer, and turned it on. I logged onto my Profyle.com. There were so many messages. I hadn't been on in some time. So many men had contacted me. I started reading through some of the messages, and most were asking for a date. In fact, some had messaged several times to ask me out.

I started out to reply to some of them, but realized I would be going back down the same road I was on when I met Anenthen. It was a road that lead to nowhere with guys who meant nothing but a night of meaningless sex. I looked at myself in the mirror hanging on the wall, and I knew I couldn't go back and become that person again when I traveled so far to discover who I was.

I hated him in that very moment and loved him at the same time. My emotions were getting the best of me, and I didn't know how to cope with all my feelings. I looked at the clock and realized it was almost four in the afternoon. I had an hour and half to get ready to meet Brackz. My eyes were so swollen, so I ran downstairs and took out a couple of ice cubes from the freezer and placed them on my eye lids to help the swelling go down. I walked back upstairs, and began to get ready for dinner.

CHAPTER FOURTEEEN

I arrived at the JW Marriott, and walked in to the lobby. I looked around and Brackz was nowhere to be found. The hotel was a sight to see. It looked like a castle from a distance, but walking in was breath taking and spectacular. I walked over to the open seating area, and sat in front of the huge open fireplace. I was twenty minutes early, so I decided to have a drink. I went over to the front desk to ask where the bar was located. I was told there were several throughout the place, but he recommended the bar and grill, High Velocity. He told me take the stairs on the left and just follow it as it would lead directly into the bar.

"Thank you."

"Are you a guest at the resort?"

"No, I'm waiting on a friend."

"I can have him paged. I just need his name."

"His name is....that's okay. I'll just wait."

I realized I didn't even know Brackz's real name. It never crossed my mind to ask him that. I could be waiting on a psychotic person who planned to kill me, and bury my body out on the golf course, and yet, there I was waiting on him. I didn't even know who he was, what his real name was, or if he even told me the truth about himself. I was in over my head, but I was already there. I could have walked away from the whole dinner thing, and just played it safe, but I was determine to find out how he knew Nia.

I proceeded to walk up the stairs and into High Velocity.

The place was nice. It had the bar set up in the middle and several open areas around it for dinning and drinking. There were several flat screen televisions throughout the place and they had every game on. But what I fell in love with was the t.v. panel that flowed in a wave pattern over the bar from one end of the wall to the other. It was like having 10 huge flat screens connected to one another. I had never seen anything like it and it was a sports fan's dream come true. I went up to sit at the bar, and ordered a glass of Mosca-to.

"That'll be fifteen dollars."

"I said a glass not a bottle."

I laughed jokingly, but I was thinking that was a steep price for a glass of Moscato even if it was a good name brand. I looked around. The place was surrounded by tourist. I assumed most were there to play golf. The resort has a PGA golf course. It was the first of its kind in San Antonio. It was located overseeing the hill country. The place was really nice, so I knew Brackz had taste. I took another sip from my glass savoring every bit of the wine as I heard my name being paged. I got up from the bar stool, and walked back over the main reception area.

As I walked up, he was standing at the front desk.

"Hi…Brackz?"

"Hola, Nova."

"I see your brushing up on your Spanish."

"Yes ma'am."

He had an accent that I had not anticipated, but I should have known that as he was from another country.

"I thought you might have backed out of the date."

"No, I was at the bar having a glass of wine. I was just a bit early."

"Is that a good thing?"

"Me being early…probably."

"Well, I wanted to tour downtown, so we can choose a restaurant down there, and thought after we can walk along y'all famous river walk. Did I get that right?"

"Yes, you did. May I ask what restaurant?"

"Any to your liking?"

"Well, I do like Fogo de Chao. Would that be okay, but we may get stuffed."

"Stuffed? Explain the meaning."

"Sorry, I forget you not from here. We could over eat at that place."

"Whatever you want is fine with me."

"Okay, shall I drive since I know the city?"

"No. I wouldn't do that to you and I want you to enjoy tonight, so I got a driver from a limousine service."

"Oh, that was cool of you. Okay, you ready?"

"I've been ready for several weeks now. Are you?"

I tried to stop from smiling, but I never could hide a smile very well. He turned to ask the attendant at the front desk if his limo was available.

"Yes sir, it's waiting for you."

"Thank you. Nova, shall we?"

My initial response was to say shall we what, but I had a feeling he wouldn't have understood the sense of humor behind it, so I just nodded my head to motion I was ready. We walked out the front doors, and there stood the limo. The driver was waiting to open the door for us. We got in and he asked if I would like something to drink. I wanted a drink to relax me, but I figured having too much to drink might be a bad idea.

"Hey Brackz, what's your name? I mean your real name."

"I wondering when you would ask me that. We been talking for months, and you agreed to meet me without even knowing my name. I was...how do you say here...blown away?"

"Yes, that's one term that could be used. Our conversations kept me interested that I never realized I didn't know your real name. I'm actually embarrassed by it."

He laughed.

"It's okay. But you are the first person I met that didn't inquire about it until the day of meeting. It's Braciano Lucas."

"Well nice to meet you...would it be okay just to keep calling you Brackz?"

"Of course Nova."

The limo arrived downtown and within minutes we were in front of the River center mall. The driver stepped out and opened our door. Brackz got out first, and as I was about to step out of the limo, he reached for my hand to help me out. I was impressed not only by his charm, but how he carried himself as a gentleman. I was wondering if I was in more trouble than I realized. We walked up to restaurant, and he opened the door for me. I smiled at him. I could definitely get use to having doors opened for me. We entered, and he asked if there was a private area in which we could be seated.

"Brackz, can we just sit amongst everyone else please?"

"Yes, I did not mean anything by it. I just wanted us to talk."

"We can, but I rather sit in the main area."

The waiter lead us to a seat located by the salad bar.

"Is this your first time here?"

"Not for me, but for my friend here...it is."

"Would you like me to explain the red and green cards."

"Sure."

The waiter then explained if you wanted the meats brought over to your table you need to have your card on green. As long as the card is on the green side, meats will continue to be brought to the table. If you don't want meats brought to you anymore, then you flip the card over to the red side. Brackz thought it was the most interesting thing.

"What may I get you both to drink?'

"I think I'll stick with Moscato tonight."

"Just a glass of water for me…thank you."

"Just water…hmmm, interesting choice."

"I'm not big on alcohol. I may have a drink later."

"Okay."

Brackz and I got up and walked over to the salad bar. Everything looked so good and so fresh. I tried a little of everything, as I always did when I went there. We went back to the table, and turned our cards over to the green side. All their meats were cooked in a Brazilian fashion, and were so good. We talked, but there was too much food coming to the table that we couldn't keep our conversation up. I realized we should have chosen a place like Ruth Chris' so we would have time to talk.

I turned my card over to the red side as I couldn't eat another bite. I definitely need a walk after such a great meal.

"Nova, would you like desert? Or another glass of wine?"

"No, thank you though, but I can't eat another bite or take another drink at this point."

"Okay then. It did look like you enjoyed each bite."

"More than you know. But the question is…did you?"

"I did. It was an interesting way to dine."

"Good, glad you could get in that experiment, I guess.
I laughed, and he smiled at me. He had a nice smile, and I was a
sucker for a nice smile.

"Shall we do this river walk thing?"

"Yes Brackz, we shall. We can just go out the door and
down the stairs, and we will be on the river walk."

"How nice."

"It's why I chose this place…we are already on the river
walk."

"Okay, let me take care of the bill and we can leave."

We left Fogo de Chao, and went down the stairs to the river
walk. He was looking at everything in sight.

"This is just a part of it. We can walk it or we can ride one
of the boats."

"Let's walk and talk Nova."

"Good idea cuz I'm so full at this point."

We walked along the path. We talked about things we
didn't know about each other. We had walked a good distance as
we reached the bridge to cross over to the other side.

"How about if we walk back on the other side?"

"That's fine."

We walked up the stairs and stop at the top of the bridge.
I looked down at the water. It was flowing along smoothly. It
brought back the memory of standing there with Maxwell the
first time we stood in that very same spot. The lights were just as
beautiful as the they were the night I stood there with Maxwell. I
remembered his smile, and his arms being around me. I could hear
him saying, "It's not about the destination, but rather who you are
going with, and the journey in which you get there." A smile came
over me. Even though Maxwell and I weren't on good terms, we

had some good times together.

"Looks like you've had some good memories here?"

"It's my home town. I have good memories just about everywhere in the city."

"Care to share?"

"Not really…hope you don't mind, but it's something long gone."

Brackz grabbed my hand and pulled in the direction of the stairs leading down to the other side of the river walk. We continue to hold a conversation about things we have done, haven't done, and would like to do. I mentioned to him that I would like to travel some day, and see parts of other countries and get a sense of all the other cultures out there. I also told him that I had a love for trying new foods from other cultures, and I was always up for doing anything once just to say I did it. He laughed at me, but said he understood where I was coming from. We walked back to the mall, our original destination, and up the stairs to find the limo awaiting us. The driver got out, but Brackz signaled for him to get back in. He opened the door for me and held me hand to lead me back into the limo. I hadn't even gotten around to asking about Nia, but I was in 'ahh' moment as he and I were having a great time. We got back to the resort.

"Nova, why don't you come upstairs with me for a drink?"

"I don't know if that's a good idea."

I had Anenthen on my mind at that point. I was still furious of how things went with him. I felt he led me on, and then ran as soon as things were getting to deep for him. He was the only guy that I left myself entirely open to and unguarded. I trusted him like no one else, and I felt betrayed. He might have been on the up and up about why he left, and I was trying to give him the benefit of the doubt, but his words kept cutting into my heart as I remembered him saying that he would never be back.

"I would never put you in a situation you would not want to be in, so if you like we can go to the bar."

"No, let's go up to your room."

"Are you sure?"

"Yes."

We walked over to the elevators, and went up to his room. He was staying in a three bedroom suite. I didn't understand that as it was only him. The suite over looked the Hill country, and it was a beautiful view. The whole place had a hacienda feel to it, but with a flare of style and sophistication. The suite had to be over 2500 square feet. It had a spacious living area, a fireplace, library, and a private master bedroom. It was bigger than the house I grew up in.

"Let's go out to the balcony. I'll get you a glass of wine."

"Only if you will joining me in that drink, Sir."

He smiled at me.

"I will."

I went out on the balcony, and the breeze felt so good on my face. It was a beautiful night out, and I could see the city lights. It was an awesome view. It was the perfect setting for romance. It would have been picture perfect for any movie setting, as it only happened in the movies. He walked out on the balcony, and over to where I was standing. He came up directly behind me, as I was standing there looking up in the night sky, and wishing over a star.

"I hope it's to your liking."

"Oh, I'm sure the wine will be."

"I was talking the scenery."

"It's beautiful."

"And yet, your beauty outshines it."

I took a sip wine. I had feeling I was going to need more than a drink with him talking like that. I knew I was so vulnerable at the moment because I was hurting, but it didn't stop me from turning around, looking into eyes, and allowing him to kiss me. I turned back around, looked out into the city lights, and took a chug of my drink.

"I could make this happen for you every day of your life."

"Make what happen?"

"This life style…whatever you dream of…I can make it happen for you."

"If I had a dollar for every time I heard that."

I laughed sarcastically. It was the first time I heard that, however, it was the second time I knew someone could give me anything I wanted. I didn't know who had more money, him or Maxwell, but the problem was, the only thing I wanted had nothing to do with materialistic things.

I took another gulp of my drink, and asked him for another. I don't know if I was trying to get drunk to take away the pain or to give myself the approval to do what I was about to do. He grabbed my glass, and walked back into the room. He came back out, and I was still standing in the same spot, still looking in the night sky.

"Would you like to get more comfortable Nova."

"Is that a way of getting me outta my clothes?"

He smiled, shook his head, and looked at me.

"Yes and No…I want you to be comfortable, but I can have them bring up something in your size more comfortable, so you would still be wearing clothing, although something you could wear to bed."

"Oh, so you plan to have me in bed before the night is

over."

"I have three bedrooms, and I don't think you should be driving...you shouldn't be driving even after one drink."

"I see...I apologize if I jumped to assumptions."

"Nova, as I said...I would never put you in a situation you don't want to be in."

"Alright, have them bring something up."

He walked over the desk phone, and had a conversation, but I was deaf to it as my mind was still somewhere else. I kept having flashes of memories. And they were coming at a rate of speed that even my mind couldn't keep up with.

"I guessed on your size, but I'm hoping red or black is your color. I'm having them bring up both."

"I don't know whether to be flattered or to proceed with caution."

"How about if you just do what comes natural."

He walked directly up to me, placed his arm around me waist, and kissed me. I was leaning against the balcony railing. A knock at the door stopped us for a moment. He grabbed my hand and lead me into the living area. I sat down while he went to answer the door. He brought back to long white boxes similar to shirt boxes.

"Open them...My opinion is I prefer the red. I see you in red."

I didn't say anything as I was not sure if I should thank him. After all, seeing me in a red negligee was more to his benefit, and he should be thanking me. I opened the first box. It was very nice and looked quite expensive. It was silk, lace, and black. I opened the second box. It was the same style, but in red. I agreed with his taste, and thought to myself that the red would look nicer on me. I grabbed both boxes and walked over to the bathroom to change. I came out, and his expression said it all.

"Breath taking."

"Wow…that's all."

"That's enough to put me out."

"So, it's all good, huh?"

"It certainly is…I'm glad you picked the red one."

I walked over to sofa, and sat down right next to him. He looked at me with the those deep, dark black eyes. I could see myself in his pupils. It was like I couldn't see him through his eyes, only my reflection. I was mesmorized just staring back at myself. We started to kiss and our hands were all over each other. I could feel his arm and thigh muscles were very toned. As I rubbed my hand over his chest and down his stomach, I could feel the crevices between each muscle in his abs. His body was a piece of artwork. And I was about to paint a beautiful picture on that canvas.

"Let's go to my room."

He took my hand and pulled me up off the sofa. He wrapped his arms around me, and walked me over to his room. He hands slip down my sides and across my stomach. He gently kissed my shoulder and made his way to my neck. I was done for it at that point. He slid the strap off of my left shoulder, and continue to kiss my neck. His hand then made way to the other strap, and he slid that one off my right shoulder. The negligee slid down my body and laid rested of the floor over me feet. He slid his hand down my back and onto my lower back area. I turned around, and put my hands on his chest, and looked up at him. He placed his hands on my hips and gently moved me to his bed. I sat down as he came closely up to me and pushed my thighs apart. I laid back and he kissed my stomach and made his way up.

"Nice mirror."

There was a mirror directly above the bed. I smiled at myself as I only saw his backside on top of me. He was still kissing my body. I was at that point of ecstasy and felt myself blacking out. I closed my eyes. Brackz had become part of me as I felt him inside. I felt his lip kissing me and then I felt a sharp pain in my neck. The same pain I felt when I woke up at Maxwell's, but this time it was so much more intense. I could feel him sucking on my neck. I opened my eyes, looked up into the mirror, and feared what I saw. My back was arched, my mouth was slightly opened from the pleasure I was feeling. The person in the mirror looked exactly like me but I could see her fangs appear as she moaned.

A flash of memories came to me, as he continued to suck away at my blood. It was like everything and every blackout moment was coming to me, the missing memories of my childhood, the time I spent with my father, my mother's spells, the night with Maxwell, and the night George died. It was crystal clear. I was the product of vampire and a brujah. It was what mom meant by I was unique and special. In that moment, my strength over came the power of Brackz, and I pushed him off of me. I looked in the mirror and saw my blood running down my neck. It was rich in its color. I wipe it off with my hand and looked at myself as if I was seeing me for the first time. Brackz sat there on the floor with a smirk on his face.

"Look at how beautiful you are."

"What did you do to me...I remember it all."

"Only what you need to be done...to remember who you are. Maxwell was a fool, he couldn't finish it because he cared for you too much. He had a soft spot for you."

"No! Why did you do this to me?"

"You are the last of your father's blood line. It's time for you to take your rightful place."

I looked at him with such hate as he sat there in such pleasure. I got up, picked up my clothes, and ran out the room. I put his shirt on as it was big enough to cover me up. I hurried to the door. He walked out,

"There's nowhere to run Nova. You can't run from who you are. I have become a part of you. I've tasted your blood, and you will be mine."

I ran out of the room and down to the elevator. He didn't come after me. The elevator opened, and I rushed in, and down to lobby. The doors opened, I made my way toward the front desk, and almost out of the fronts doors, but something stopped me from walking out. I turned and there stood Maxwell. He looked at me and started to walk toward me. Tears ran down as I backed up slowly.

"Nova, wait!"

I turned and ran. The front doors of the resort opened up. I was barefoot, but nothing I stepped on was as painful as the hurt I was feeling in my heart. I was playing back all the images I saw as I laid there with Brackz on top of me. I felt so betrayed by everyone as they all knew who or rather what I was and not one of them told me anything. The most pain came from knowing that my own mom knew and she failed to enlighten me. The only people I could trust at this point were my sorority sisters and Anenthen. How was I going to tell my sisters about this? How was I going to find Anenthen, and did he want to be found?

I got to my car, got in, and sped away. I drove for miles. Everything was becoming so clear. The biggest question on my mind was how did I forget something that big and important in my life. How do you not know who you truly are? How do you block out so much and why? I knew the only person that could give me these answers was an hour away, and I was heading in that direction.

As I was driving down highway 281 and toward my mom's house, my cell phone rang. It was Tee's ringtone.

"Hey Tee, what's up?"

"We just heard from Luna and Mrs. Carmichael."

"Did they find Nia?"

"They're not really sure."

"What do you mean?"

"She was seen at several locations, and the last place see was seen, she was with a male companion."

"I still don't understand what you mean by they're not really sure."

"They didn't see her personally. She, the female, was captured on video surveillance in stores, restaurants, etc. But her face was not captured on any of the tapes. Mrs. Carmichael was certain it was Nia, but Luna wasn't so sure."

"Where was the last place she was seen?"

"At the airport, and she was seen boarding a flight. They checked the flight list, and her name came up on a passenger flight to Houston, Texas."

"Tee, it has to be Nia…it just has to be. I have a feeling that she is okay."

"Where are you at?"

"Tee…"

I grew silent on the phone.

"Nova, what's wrong?"

"Tee, I gotta go…we need to talk though."

I hung up the phone before she could ask me anything. I continued to head in the direction to seek the answers I was looking for.

www.ingramcontent.com/pod-product-compliance
Lightning Source LLC
Chambersburg PA
CBHW030305180626
46810CB00003B/932